EBURY PRESS
VICHHODA

Harinder Sikka has been with Piramal Enterprises Ltd for nearly three decades. He is currently the group director, strategic business. After graduating from Delhi University, he joined Indian Navy in 1979 and was commissioned in January 1981. He took premature retirement in 1993 as lieutenant commander.

He produced a film, *Nanak Shah Fakir*, in 2015 on the life and teachings of Guru Nanak. The film won acclaim at the international film festivals in Cannes, Toronto and Los Angeles and was also screened at the Rashtrapati Bhavan by the then honourable President of India, Pranab Mukherjee. The film won three national awards, including the most coveted Nargis Dutt Award for best feature film on national integration.

Calling Sehmat, his first book, was a national bestseller and has been published in many Indian languages. The book was also made into a film titled *Raazi*, starring Alia Bhatt, and was a box office success.

Sikka lives in New Delhi with his family.

Harinder Sikka

VICHHODA

In the shadow of longing...

EBURY
PRESS

An imprint of Penguin Random House

EBURY PRESS

USA | Canada | UK | Ireland | Australia
New Zealand | India | South Africa | China

Ebury Press is part of the Penguin Random House group of companies
whose addresses can be found at global.penguinrandomhouse.com

Published by Penguin Random House India Pvt. Ltd.
4th Floor, Capital Tower 1, MG Road,
Gurugram 122 002, Haryana, India

First published in Ebury Press by Penguin Random House India 2019

ISBN 9780143447306

Typeset in Adobe Garamond Pro by Manipal Technologies Limited, Manipal
Printed at Replika Press Pvt. Ltd, India

www.penguin.co.in

To my parents and Ajay G. Piramal

1

'Kill the Kafirs, burn them alive. No Hindu or Sikh should be spared . . .' Hate-filled directives echoed in the Valley as young and old Muslim men ran through the narrow streets of Tadali village in Muzaffarabad, Kashmir, with naked, bloodstained swords in their hands. The village was to become part of Pakistan post Partition. The vicious venom being spewed by the local mullahs had brainwashed the Muslim youth almost overnight and filled them with hatred towards communities of other religions. With no regulatory body to be afraid of, the fundamentalists went on killing sprees with full gusto. It was as if some evil force had swished a magic wand and turned friends and immediate neighbours into arch-enemies. They sprinted out of their homes like pit bulls freed from chains and

1

filled the Valley with the blood of innocents, leaving a burning trail of houses in their wake. They marched on to the streets like wild beasts, displaying human skulls as trophies on the tips of their spears and swords.

The Sikhs provoked the ire of the fundamentalists even more. Being entrepreneurs, they had earned respect and jealousy in equal proportions. Despite being limited in number, they dominated all of Punjab and firmly held the purse strings of the important businesses. Even though Muslims benefited the most from their entrepreneurial skills, they remained discontent. They had been waiting for an opportunity to strike back. The word 'Jihad' acquired a new meaning. Instead of being a spiritual struggle to overcome ego, greed and lust, it was wrongly interpreted as the Prophet's directive to wage wars against non-Muslims and used to justify the killing of innocent people.

One Sikh family that suffered the most at their hands was that of Balwant Singh. Being the eldest of four brothers, Balwant had successfully expanded the business and taken it to great heights. Nearly one-third of the village population was under his direct or indirect employment. His palatial home was famously known as 'Sardar House', and he was treated no less than a king. He was a large-hearted man and gave soft loans to anyone in distress without discriminating on the basis of caste or creed, or worrying about returns. Spiritually inclined, Balwant donated a fixed percentage of his income to noble causes every month and took good care of anyone who knocked on his door. Yet, the Muslim clergy nursed a serious grudge against him. His big white house stood out like a sore thumb primarily for one reason— his school for the underprivileged. Balwant enjoyed generous patronage of the local British administrators and, as a result, was permitted to run a prominent 'girls only' school in the Valley. The school encouraged poor children, including Muslim girls, to study free of cost which became a bone of contention for the religious leaders who were of the opinion that educating Muslim girls was against the teachings of the Quran.

However, over a period of time, the school gained a name for its good governance, discipline and education. Despite being located in a Muslim area, it boasted a high percentage of Muslim students, which the fundamentalists found difficult to digest, and thus they opposed it vehemently. But the wealthy and powerful Balwant brushed their objections aside each time and kept them at a safe distance. They were enraged by the snub but also scared to stand up to the powerful sardar and hence sulked in isolation. The British administration was uncompromising when it came to rules. Punishments for disobedience and violence were severe and dispensed quickly. Hence, whenever the pitch of their murmur rose above the acceptable decibel level, Balwant reminded them of the Riot Act. But his trust in the

British administration was his undoing. He was unaware of the level of hatred that was brewing in the minds of the imams, moulvis and other fundamentalists. The sudden announcement of Partition brought all these feelings to the fore, and without the British police to regulate the town, they wreaked vengeance. Their leaders used loudspeakers in masjids to spew hatred. The volcano of hate exploded and the burning lava flowed in the direction of the Sardar House. It took Balwant by complete surprise and engulfed his entire family.

This was hard for Balwant to digest. Even in his wildest dreams, he had not imagined that his own Muslim friends, especially those who had taken umpteen favours and had sworn by him, would lead a riotous mob in the direction of his house. They were holding weapons, hurling abuses and baying for his blood. Panic-stricken and in deep shock, he quickly gathered his entire family of twelve, which included his three brothers, their wives and children, including four teenage daughters, into one room and bolted it from inside. Being the eldest, he stood with his back to the front door. That's when he saw their horrified faces. Things had escalated so quickly that none of them had had the time to contemplate. It was only then they understood the gravity of the situation and the danger they were in. The look on Balwant's face distressed them even more. 'I have helped each one of these mullahs for decades, given them rock-solid support in their times of need. And today they have declared us enemies because we are not Muslims? Just because some gora sitting in his plush office in London has drawn a vague line on the map? These select traitors have put a blot on the entire Muslim community. How are we to ever trust each other again?' Balwant muttered.

Meanwhile, with every passing moment, the chorus outside was growing louder, adding to the tension and fear. Balwant peeped out from the small window and saw hundreds of rioters flashing burning torches. In the background, he could see other Hindu houses being looted and burnt. The brainwashed crowd was mercilessly chopping the heads and other body parts of the Hindus, leaving cries, screams and flames behind. He could hear chants of 'Allahu Akbar!' The shouting brigade soon reached Balwant Singh's home, and in a single attempt broke down the tall steel gate. Within moments, they reached the strong teakwood entrance door and began beating the polished structure with spears, hammers and swords.

'We shall fight!' said Balwant hurriedly to his brothers in a voice that was shaky with emotions but firm. 'Let no one be taken alive,' he continued and looked at his wife, Priti, who rushed to his side. Tears rolled down her cheeks.

'Please kill us all first. Make sure that no girl is left alive to be raped by these bastards. Please, Balwant, are you listening?' she said, pummelling her husband's chest with her fists.

Balwant froze on hearing these words. He looked at his wife in disbelief, mentally mustering up the courage to take the dreadful step. He knew he didn't have a lot of time as the front door had begun to shake violently, threatening to collapse any moment. Balwant walked towards his brothers, folded his hands and said in a polite tone, 'If this is what Waheguru demands of us, then so be it. We shall comply.'

The chants outside grew louder as the mob became more restless and violent. Huddled together, the family members joined their hands to say their last prayer. Outside, a new conspiracy was brewing. Unable to break down the strong wooden door, the mob had decided to set the house on fire. By the time the family finished its prayers, the house was engulfed in flames. The brothers raised their swords and screamed the battle cry, *Jo bole so nihal, Sat Sri Akal* [He who chants the lord's name stays blessed]!' Then, with tears rolling down their cheeks, they slashed at their daughters with weapons. One by one, all the teenage girls fell to the ground and lay in pools of blood. The middle-aged women came next. They cried out aloud, wept bitterly and shut their eyes in pain. Each one of them knew the consequences of being taken alive.

After the last woman had been slain, the brothers took a step back and looked at the bodies lying on the floor, their faces pale, their eyes brimming with tears. However, there was no time to mourn or even get into a huddle. Soon, the burning door came crashing down and fell inwards, letting the rioters into the courtyard. Not finding anyone there, they started banging on the door of the room where the family had locked itself in. The brothers shouted the battle cry once again, '*Jo bole so nihal* . . .' and launched a fierce counter-attack. They thrust and slashed at their enemies with their swords, killing the first set of attackers. The second, third and fourth lot met the same fate. But the rioters kept pouring in. The communal bloodbath continued till Balwant and his brothers were stabbed to death. An eerie silence descended over the house after the carnage was over. The floor was covered with dead bodies, severed limbs and a thick layer of blood.

Zarif Islam, the oldest fanatic leader amongst the mullahs, stepped forward and glanced at the heap of human flesh. He was taken aback by the unexpected retaliation and was angry to see so many of his men killed by just a handful of untrained Sikhs. His hate-filled eyes scanned the spacious hall and stopped when they saw a familiar face. The dead boy was lying under a broken table, his legs partially hidden under the heap. Suddenly something struck him. *Was it?* Zarif recognized the bold stripes on the long shirt. Hoping against hope, he quickly bent down and with some effort pushed aside the wooden table which was blocking his view. It was his own son, Anwar, lying in a pool of blood! His eyes popped out as excruciating pain shot through his chest. He fell on the floor, writhing in agony. Others came running and tried to calm him down but failed. His loud screams echoed in the empty hall. He held his son's face and placed it on his lap. 'My own son has sacrificed himself fighting the Kafirs for the sake of our faith. No Sikh or Hindu should be left alive in the Valley. Get rid of them all, kill them, burn them, destroy them, now! Leave me alone. Go, go, go!' he screamed.

The mob acknowledged his words in unison and, following the mullah's dictate, began exiting in a hurry. They rushed towards the next building, fire torches in hand, and set it alight. Having had their fill, they moved on, and the street was once again engulfed in silence. In the distance, one could hear the shrill battle cry, but other than that, there was only the stillness of death and dying.

Zarif sat numbly next to his son's body and continued to sob uncontrollably. It is said that no pain is greater than losing one's child. At this point, he had completely forgotten his own cruelty and was absorbed in his misery which seemed unique to him. 'Didn't I tell you to stay home? But you didn't listen to me. Now see what has happened. O Allah, what have I done to deserve this? Why couldn't you have some mercy on me? What will I do now?

Anwar was my only child. How will I live without him?' he wailed, but there was no one to hear his cries.

Meanwhile, the raging fire had spread to other parts of the house. It had swallowed the wooden furniture and other inflammable materials. Realizing the extent of the danger he was in, Zarif tried to stand up in a hurry but slipped and fell on his face. His clothes were soaked in blood that his followers had shed. It now struck him that he could be the next victim of this fire. Shaken and scared, he somehow managed to stand up and run towards the door, trampling the dead bodies under his feet. He reached the exit but slipped again and fell on the broken wooden door that was drenched in kerosene oil. His clothes caught fire, and in no time he was aflame.

He ran out with his hands up in the air and cried out aloud. His screams echoed wildly across the Valley, merging with the hundreds of other painful cries. His followers were too busy looting, burning and killing in the name of Allah, the merciful.

There was no help for the one who'd killed in the name of God . . .

2

As dawn broke, the sunrays lit up the blackened, half-burnt structure of what was once Balwant Singh's palatial haveli. Moulvi Syed Zade, Balwant's old friend and neighbour, stepped into the broken house with the help of his walking stick. '*Ya Khuda!*' he exclaimed in deep pain and horror as he walked past the mutilated bodies. His eyes brimmed with tears as he scanned the room and saw the destruction. He bent down to take a closer look at the faces which had escaped the fire. The hurt and pain deepened the wrinkles on his face. The lifeless bodies of the two young boys in green and red shirts were his sons'. He touched their faces one by one and felt their pulse. The sword hanging loosely from one of their hands rolled out on to the wooden floor. With some difficulty, he managed to stand up, looked at the dead faces of his sons again and spoke in a soft but firm tone, 'I didn't expect you both to become such savages.

I am ashamed to call you my sons. I regret to say that you don't even deserve a respectful burial for the heinous crimes you have committed. What face will you show Allah? Is this what Islam has taught you?' He shook his head in disapproval.

Then, with some effort, he started walking towards the broken door, manoeuvring around the bodies. Blood had coagulated on the floor and become a thick, dark-brownish-maroon paste that stuck to his shoes each time he stepped forward. Most of the furniture and over a dozen bodies were burnt beyond recognition. Pinching his nostrils, he was about to exit when he heard a soft, pain-ridden voice. He halted, turned and carefully looked around again. He saw a body move slightly. He walked closer to where the sound was coming from and found a teenage girl writhing and moaning. She was badly wounded and unable to move. He rushed to her side and checked her pulse—she was alive. A moment later, using all his strength, he lifted her up. He put his right arm beneath her left and let her head gently rest on his right shoulder. He cautiously walked out with his delicate load on to the empty street which was engulfed in deathly silence. He tiptoed to his house and managed to get inside safely without anyone noticing them. He took her to the living room and put her on the cot. Then he went back to the door and through the peephole carefully scanned the houses around. Satisfied that no one was watching him, he locked the door and went back in.

Bibi Amrit Kaur, the beautiful teenage daughter of his best friend, was breathing, albeit heavily. He rushed to the kitchen and came back with a pot of warm water. Using pieces of cloth, he cleaned the wounds on her arms and shoulders. He looked at her injuries carefully. He could see a deep gash on her neck that had been bleeding profusely and now had a chunk of dried blood on it. Syed dipped the cloth in warm water again and cleaned the lesion very slowly and carefully. He then went to the kitchen and brought a tray containing three copper bowls of various sizes and shapes filled with turmeric powder, mustard oil and hot water. Like most elderly villagers, Syed too was well versed in home-made remedies and knew about the antiseptic qualities of turmeric. He put the hot oil and turmeric powder in equal proportions into the copper vessel, stirred the mixture and then ran a thread through the thick, yellow paste. He then sterilized the needle by placing it in the same mixture. She whimpered when he lifted her head and placed another pillow under it, but remained in a semi-conscious state.

Syed looked up and said a small prayer, asking Allah to give him the strength to do what he was about to and that it be beneficial for her. Then, using the needle and thread he had just sterilized, he began sewing the two ends of the gash. Tiny drops of blood oozed out each time the needle entered from one end and emerged from the other. Syed knew that if she was awake, this would have been very painful. The dim light from the bedside lamp was not enough and he had to squint to see clearly. She was badly injured and many of her body parts bore signs of the assault. She had lost a lot of blood and her chances of survival looked bleak. But Syed Zade was not one to give up. He tirelessly attended to her injuries and painstakingly applied the turmeric concoction on her wounds. Two hours later, he stood up and looked at his work. His back was aching but his eyes had an expression of satisfaction. He covered the wounds with betel leaves and wrapped them in shreds that came from a torn bed sheet. This was all he could do. This and pray.

His eyes were shut but his lips were moving; he was asking the biggest doctor of the universe to intervene. When she developed a fever, he wiped her forehead and palms with cold water to bring the temperature down.

Bibi remained unconscious the next day as well, but her fever did not come back. Syed didn't leave her side. Almost twenty hours later, in the middle of the night, she opened her eyes and became conscious of the extreme soreness and pain in her neck. She stared at the ceiling for a few minutes and then turned her gaze towards Syed. She recognized him and tried to speak but only tears rolled down her cheeks. She couldn't move her head; her lips were parched and flaky. 'Kill me, Baba . . .' she whispered as fresh tears filled her eyes. 'I don't want to live . . . Please, let me go to my parents . . .' she sobbed. Syed noticed that she was straining the muscles of her neck to talk. The deep gash on her neck, which Syed had somehow stitched together, was threatening to reopen, and the excruciating pain was making her faint.

He immediately held her face and looked into her eyes to calm her down. Then he sat next to her and held her hands. He was so shaken by her words that he couldn't hold back his tears. He hadn't spoken to anyone about his ordeal in the past two days, and now that there was someone to share, his patience broke too. 'Forgive me, my child, for the crimes that my sons have committed . . . I beg you,' he said with folded hands. 'I am ashamed and deeply embarrassed. This is not what the holy Quran teaches us.' Syed paused, wiped his tears with the back of his hand and continued, 'I am also grateful to Allah that instead of the two wretched rascals whom I thought were my real sons, he has blessed me with an angel like you. I request you to accept me as your father. Get well soon and we shall move out of this godforsaken village to my ancestral home in Muzaffarabad. I don't wish to live here even for a minute longer than we have to. But till then, please stay calm and somehow tolerate the unbearable pain.'

However, Bibi's tears refused to recede. The inhuman and barbaric acts of people, who till a day before had been close friends, had shaken and shattered her faith completely. She sobbed inconsolably. Syed fed her some water, after which she fell unconscious again. He covered her with a bed sheet and fanned her forehead. 'Please forgive me, Allah, forgive me for the crimes my sons have committed. Give me strength to bring up Bibi as my own daughter, I beg of you. Help me heal her heart so that she can stand on her feet again,' he prayed. Then, taking a piece of cloth and dipping it in hot water, he gently sponged her forehead and arms. He also slid small spoons of honey mixed with milk through her lips and repeatedly checked her pulse. He prayed each time after doing so.

The sharp afternoon sun gave way to the soft hues of dusk but the old man refused to give up. As the sun set behind the mountains, Bibi opened her eyes again to find Syed by her side, looking at her with hope. He muttered a quick prayer to thank Allah and then addressed her softly, 'Allah, the almighty, wants you to live, my child, and emerge stronger from this unfortunate incident. We have a long journey ahead. Don't give up. Be brave, my girl. Get well soon. We are surrounded by wretched beasts in the garb of humans. We will leave this place as soon as you're slightly better.' She didn't respond; instead, she closed her eyes and rested her head on the pillow. The pain in her eyes was far greater than that of the near fatal wounds she had on her body.

The next two days were no less demanding. It became difficult for Syed to keep Bibi's presence in his home a secret. His indifference towards the death of his sons had set tongues wagging. Many people in the neighbourhood, especially the youth, began gossiping. They wanted to know why the old man had not attended the burials of his own sons. Syed never left Bibi alone and made sure that the front door of his house always remained bolted from inside. Even if he had to step out for a few minutes, he made sure he pulled the old latch and secured it with a big lock. Though the bloodbath in the neighbourhood had ended, he could still hear battle cries from the burning houses in other villages. His peaceful Valley was bleeding profusely but he couldn't do anything. Sitting like a helpless, lame duck, he waited impatiently for Bibi to recover—enough to undertake the long journey. The frequent application of the turmeric concoction on her wounds had turned his fingertips yellow. His white shirt too bore innumerable stains. But the old man knew that it was a do-or-die situation. His body was weak, but his spirit was strong enough to fight the brutes.

Bibi had lost a lot of blood. As a result, she kept slipping in and out of consciousness but miraculously didn't sink into a coma—it was probably Syed's prayers and efforts that kept her alive. After two days of extensive care, Bibi finally began showing signs of recovery. But her moans grew louder. The neighbourhood was aware that he did not have a daughter, only two sons who had been killed in the riots. His wife had also passed away several years ago. It therefore became difficult for Syed to keep Bibi's identity a secret.

His immediate neighbour, Iqbal, even questioned him about the cries but Syed said nothing, which made his neighbour even more suspicious. They were not the best of friends, but out of sheer respect for his aged neighbour, Iqbal decided to keep his eyes and ears shut. He, however, was aware that there were others who weren't as tolerant. As Bibi's painful moaning grew louder, more people began to wonder. Iqbal couldn't take it any more and decided to talk to Syed.

One evening, he went to Syed's house and said, 'Bhaijaan, there could be an attack on you after the first azan in the wee hours. I advise you to shift the patient to my house. Give her an extra dosage so that she sleeps well. I will organize a bullock cart. You should move out of Tadali as soon as possible.'

Left with no other choice, Syed nodded and did as he was told.

As promised, in the middle of the night, Iqbal arrived at Syed's doorstep on a bullock cart. With great haste, the two men shifted Bibi into the cart and carefully positioned her on the right side of the vehicle. They covered the left portion with a haystack and closed the canvas hood. The two men mounted the cart from the front and pushed the bulls forward. Dawn was still a few hours away, but men with fire torches were keeping a vigil, ready to hack any Hindu family attempting to flee. Iqbal skilfully manoeuvred the cart through the narrow lanes and kept it away from the prying eyes till they reached the highway. It became clear to Syed that Iqbal had done his homework well before undertaking the risk. Once out of danger, Iqbal stepped down from the cart and bid Syed goodbye with a bear hug.

When Iqbal reached home, he saw over a dozen hooligans assembled outside Syed's home. The mullah of the village mosque, Maulana Javed Hussein, was leading them. Each one of them was holding a fire torch. They saw Iqbal approaching but didn't seem to care. On a cue from the mullah, they screamed 'Allahu Akbar!' a few times and broke open the front door. Finding no one inside, they threw their torches at the walls, setting the house on fire, and came out dancing, filling the air with their rants. The mullah looked at Iqbal, raised his right hand, smiled and said, 'Your neighbour was a Kafir, Iqbal Bhai. And there's no room for such people in Allah's land.' His face was lit with self-glorification.

Iqbal took a few steps towards the mullah. He was seething with rage. 'Did Allah come to your home, Maulana, to give this advice? If even a single blade of grass on my premises catches fire, I will ensure you burn along with it!' he screamed. A flabbergasted Maulana saw the anger-filled expression on Iqbal's face and the naked steel blade tied to his waist and took a step back.

He then turned to his followers and shouted loudly, 'Douse the fire, you idiots, douse the fire! Iqbal Bhai's house is in danger!'

The stunned followers looked first at Maulana and then at Iqbal. Given his standing in the community, it didn't take them much time to understand the consequences of his threat. They scampered about and began throwing bucketfuls of water at Syed's home. A sheepish Maulana hurriedly slipped away, leaving behind his followers to face Iqbal's wrath.

Meanwhile, the two sturdy bullocks trotted the whole night and, after a brief rest in an empty, discarded barn, reached Muzaffarabad the next day, which by then had been occupied by the Pakistani armed forces. Far away from Syed's riotous home, Sadali was much more peaceful, calm and serene. He shifted Bibi to his sister Zaida's home and, after a day's rest, headed back to his village. On his way home, he stopped to give back the bullock cart to its rightful owner and walked the rest of the distance.

However, a rude shock awaited him. The door to his house was ajar. On closer inspection, he realized that the lock had been smashed and all his belongings were lying scattered on the floor and some were even half burnt. The word 'Kafir' was scrawled on a placard in black ink and hung on the wall. Syed smiled to himself, raised his hands, looked up towards the sky and said, '*Mein Kafir achha aise panj namaazian to, tera shukar hai mere Rabba, lakh-lakh shukar hai mere Khuda* [I am better a Kafir than those who say namaz five times a day. I am grateful to you, O Lord, thankful to you, O Allah].'

He turned towards the door to find a giant shadow blocking the entrance with a naked sword in hand. The bright sunlight streaming in made it difficult for Syed to recognize the intruder. He looked carefully. It was Iqbal. They stood in silence for a few seconds, admiring each other, before Iqbal stepped forward and broke the ice. 'I have seen hundreds of maulanas shouting Allah from atop mosques. But today, I feel fortunate to be standing in front of a true Sufi. Please pardon me, Syed Sahib. I doubted you and didn't recognize the godliness you radiate,' he said as the sword fell from his hand with a loud clang. Syed didn't say a word. Instead, he took a step forward and embraced Iqbal.

He was crying. 'Thank you, Iqbal, for saving my daughter,' he managed to whisper.

Over the next few days, Syed behaved like he had lost his mind due to the sudden death of his two young sons and the rude behaviour of the villagers. He began wandering aimlessly and acted like a madman. He misbehaved with shopkeepers, scattered their wares, broke glass tumblers at tea kiosks and hurled abuses at passers-by. Out of guilt, sympathy and pity, the villagers tolerated his behaviour but soon became wary of his presence. On the fifth day, Syed set his own house on fire and began dancing in the veranda outside. The villagers rushed to his rescue. This performance convinced the mullahs that he wasn't sheltering any non-Muslims in his house. On the sixth day, Syed woke up early, stepped out of what was left of his semi-burnt home, bid goodbye to Iqbal and began his long walk towards his ancestral home.

After a few hours on the highway, he spotted a bus and waved it down frantically. The driver applied his brakes and allowed him to board the bus. After a few hours, Syed reached Zaida's home at Sadali. Two days later he moved into a new home nearby and began his life afresh with his adopted daughter. Time sped by, and, with that, to some extent, it also healed Bibi's heart.

Syed looked after Bibi better than a parent. He brought her up without forcing her to change her name or religion. She began to be known by her nickname, 'Bibi', and mostly remained under the protective cover of a veil. Her new life was filled with simple, honest hill people and the small joys of life. This is when she realized how religious leaders abused and brainwashed the common man in the name of Islam for power, wealth and fame. She compared Syed, a pious Muslim, with the hundreds of Islam followers in Tadali who actively participated in riots in the name of Allah. She once overheard Zaida questioning Syed and demanding reasons for not attending the burial ceremony of his own sons. Her respect for her adopted father grew manifold.

Slowly but surely, her scars began to heal, and an occasional smile could be seen on her face. Over time, the bond of trust and faith between the two strengthened and they started looking after each other. Bibi began to accept the whole episode as part of her destiny and to recover from her painful past. Bibi spent most of her time looking after the ageing Syed, knowing that his health was deteriorating with every passing day. She knew that somewhere deep within, he was unable to forgive himself for not attending his sons' funeral. She therefore left no stone unturned to keep her father happy. And soon, they started making new memories together.

About a year later, Syed married Bibi to his brother's son. His own failing health was one of the reasons for hastening the wedding. Sakhiullah, a well-to-do, thorough gentleman, was made aware of Bibi's background and the challenging conditions she was brought up in. He empathized with the pain she had suffered during and post Partition. Soon, the two began their life together. Within a year of their marriage, Syed passed away, bequeathing all his possessions to Bibi Amrit Kaur.

Over the next three years, Bibi was blessed with two sons named Qasim Zaid and Karim Zaid. The presence of two beautiful children further helped Bibi lead a normal, happy life. Sakhiullah was gainfully employed and looked after the needs of his family well. Besides, he was also respected by his neighbours and others in the village as he was prosperous and contributed to the community. As a result, Bibi too was treated with respect. Married at a young age, her breathtaking beauty attracted many admirers. Her helpful nature and kind-heartedness made her a leader amongst the women in the community. Despite her troubled and devastating past, Bibi pulled her life together and started afresh.

3

In 1950, after three years of Partition, the prime ministers of the two warring nations, Liaquat Ali Khan and Jawaharlal Nehru, signed a treaty which gave freedom to the women of both countries to return home. Bibi opted to stay back in Pakistan as her world revolved around her two beautiful children and doting husband. But destiny had something else in store for her. Even though Bibi had mostly confined herself to the four walls of her home, word of her mesmerizing and breathtaking sharp features had spread in the region. Given her marital status and the enormous respect her husband commanded, no one had dared cast an evil eye on her. Yet, there were men who never missed an opportunity to look at her discreetly and sigh lustfully.

Following the government's directives, the station house officer (SHO) of the district issued orders to all villages, directing the women of Indian origin to confirm in writing their decision—live in Sadali as Pakistani citizens or return to India. Sakhiullah was away on a business tour for a few days. Bibi read the circular and signed the documents, confirming Muzaffarabad in Pakistan as her choice of residence. The havildar, who came to collect the document, was awestruck by Bibi's beauty—her sharp but delicate features, porcelain skin and petite figure. He found it difficult to take his eyes off her and was filled with desire. Sensing his intention, she picked up her children and rushed inside. Her behaviour rebuffed him for the time being. However, the havildar couldn't stop thinking about her. Back in the police station, he recounted the incident to his colleagues.

Unknown to the havildar, the SHO, Irfan Chaudhary, was eavesdropping on his poetic description of Bibi's exquisite features. He was so intrigued by what he heard that he felt compelled to see her. The next day he drove all the way to Bibi's home and knocked at her door. Bibi opened the door—her head covered, her nine-month-old son resting in her lap. Their eyes met. He had not seen anyone quite as pretty, elegant and desirable as Bibi. Recovering somewhat, he managed to ask for her residential status. By now, Bibi had sensed something in his reaction as well. She responded uncomfortably, 'My husband is coming home tonight. He will personally come to your office tomorrow and complete all the formalities.'

The SHO smiled shamelessly, enjoying the many shades of pink that were appearing on Bibi's face in quick succession. 'No, no,' he replied with an intention to extend the dialogue. 'I don't want to bother your husband. This is just a small formality, yet it must be completed at the earliest. There's a police chowki in this village itself. You can come and sign the documents and be done with it. That will close the matter once and for all. Now that you are legally married to a Pakistani national and have two sons, the formalities won't take much time,' he added slyly.

Bibi was perplexed. She tried to think and then looked at the SHO's face, who smiled hopefully and repeated, 'It has to be done today, Bibi, otherwise I wouldn't have troubled you. Please have mercy on me. There are many more homes to go to.'

Bibi couldn't think of a suitable excuse. She had no choice but to go to the police chowki within the next hour. The SHO left, smiling cunningly.

Bibi hurriedly finished her daily chores and discussed the matter with the elderly women in her locality. Given the circumstances, she felt it was best to consult others as well. At their advice, she requested her next-door neighbour to babysit for her. However, another neighbour decided to accompany her to the police station. Bibi felt relieved that she wasn't going alone. A local tonga was hired and the two burqa-clad women reached the police chowki, which was located on the outskirts of the village. To their surprise, they found a policeman eagerly waiting for Bibi's arrival. However, seeing an elderly woman accompanying her, he stopped them at the entrance and went inside the small, makeshift chowki. They waited. A short while later, the policeman came out again. He walked towards the duo and asked the elderly lady to wait outside while he took Bibi inside to sign the papers.

This seemed reasonable enough, so Bibi went in. She found the SHO sitting across a table—his eyes glued on Bibi, as if trying to pierce through the black veil. A bunch of papers and an inkpot with two wooden pens dipped in the holder were lying on the right side of the large wooden desk. Bibi sensed his intentions and grew uncomfortable. The SHO quickly removed one of the pens from the inkpot and placed it in front of Bibi. She hurriedly signed the documents without even reading them. Then she stood up in a hurry and was about to leave when the SHO rushed to the door and bolted it from inside.

'Bibi,' he said, looking at her lustfully. 'What you have just signed is sufficient for me to send you back to Hindustan. It says that you're not interested in living in Pakistan and would like to go back to your country. But if you do wish to live here, then spend the next hour with me . . . I'll make sure you stay here with your sons and their father, or else . . .' he looked straight at her. 'It's up to you. Decide quickly.'

Bibi was astounded. She could not believe what she had just heard. Then fear took over. Her heart started pounding in her chest, and she cried and pleaded for mercy. But the lust-driven cop was in no mood to relent; he was not going to give up the golden goose so easily. He strode towards her and held her tightly by her arms. Bibi retracted her arms but, while doing so, fell on her back on the table. She let out a loud scream and then burst into tears. The constable standing outside on watch heard her screams but didn't have the guts to interfere. He pretended that he had not heard a thing. However, soon her screams could be heard till the road. The old woman rushed over and tried to intervene, but she was forcefully stopped by the same havildar. He threatened her with dire consequences and angrily pushed her in the direction of the tonga. Seeing the commotion, the horseman came running to help the old woman. But he too was abused and threatened by the cop. 'Return to Sadali or I will put you behind bars!' barked the sentry.

Helpless and scared, the horseman drove the tonga away from the police station and parked it on the other side of the road. Then, stepping down from the tonga, he sat on the tarmac and began praying for Bibi's safety.

The elderly woman joined him, and together they sought heavenly intervention for Bibi's safe return. At the police chowki, the havildar saw the tonga pulling over, but except for frantically waving his hand and directing the tonga driver to go away, he couldn't do anything.

Inside the chowki, Bibi was struggling to free herself from the SHO's grip. Scenes from Partition flashed in front of her eyes. In the SHO, she saw the rioters and fundamentalists who, in order to fulfil their greed and lust, had stooped to the lowest of the low and exploited innocent people to show their strength and power. And right then she made up her mind to not give in and fight back. With her back on the table, she searched for a sharp object to attack the SHO with her right hand. Her desperate efforts yielded results and she managed to get hold of the wooden pen. She pulled it out of the inkpot and, with all her strength, thrust it deep into the SHO's left eye. The sharp, one-inch-long nib pierced his eye and got stuck inside, the ink flowing down his cheek, colouring it blue-black. It was soon followed by thick blood. The SHO let out a loud scream and collapsed. He fell on his face, allowing the nib to go even deeper inside the eye socket.

He screamed again. Then he somehow turned on his back and shouted for help. The startled havildar couldn't make out what was happening. He panicked and rushed towards the door but found it locked from inside. He looked around but found no one in the vicinity to help. It soon dawned on him that the SHO had sent away all the cops on duty to fulfil his lust. He ran towards the road and screamed at the top of his voice in the direction of the horseman and the old woman, but saw them kneeling on the ground in prayer. He again ran towards the door and tried desperately to force it open but failed. Left with no other choice, he banged on the door with his bare hands. The screams from inside kept growing louder, both in pitch and intensity. Unable to bear it any more and fearing the wrath of his senior, the helpless havildar ran towards the houses at the far end, shouting loudly en route, 'Somebody help, please help . . .' But the few who did hear him looked the other way lest they get drawn into the messy affairs of cops.

Meanwhile, inside the chowki, a furious Bibi couldn't contain herself. All the anger and anguish came out in the most vicious manner. Free from the SHO's grip, she looked for the document she had signed, tore it and flung the pieces on the body of the injured cop. His uniform had soaked up the blood that had oozed from his eye initially but was now forming a pool under his head. Her eyes still on the cop, who was writhing in pain, she tugged at the tablecloth and wiped her hands—her face lit with satisfaction. Gone was the begging, pleading woman. Instead she looked at the cop coldly, not heeding his sobs and pleas.

Having suffered immensely at the hands of such rogues not too long ago, she was in the mood to settle scores. She walked resolutely towards the cop and with all her strength kicked him in the groin. He screamed again and doubled over in pain—his right hand gripping his vitals, his body writhing. Bibi waited for him to settle in one posture for a few minutes. Then she walked towards the other end of the room and lifted the flowerpot kept close to the wall. She walked back and waited. The SHO had turned on his back again. She held the pot over him and dropped it on his groin with full force. The pot broke into many pieces. The injuries caused by the shards made the cop cough up blood and lose consciousness.

Bibi stared at him for signs of activity, then, not finding any, dusted her hands, walked towards the door, opened the latch and flung it open. The havildar had gone to get help, so he wasn't there to catch her. Not that she cared. Without showing any signs of hurry, she quietly stepped out and shut the door firmly behind her. After a brief pause, she removed her burqa, which had bloodstains from the struggle, smoothened her hair, wiped her dried tears and turned towards the door. She found a lock hanging from it. She pulled it out and latched and bolted the door. 'Thank you, Waheguru,' she said softly and then began walking towards the tonga that seemed farther up than she'd left it.

She saw the old woman and the horseman rushing towards her. 'Are you okay, Bibi?' they inquired. It was now the old woman's turn to be surprised as she gazed at her stern, anger-filled expression.

'Yes, Badi Bee,' Bibi said evenly. I'm fine, and everyone else will be fine, because the SHO will never look at any woman lustfully.'

As she sat in the tonga, her face was calm, composed and bereft of worries and fear of the far-reaching consequences of her actions.

4

The constable rushed back to see the tonga leaving. He had not found any help nearby. He was perplexed to see the burqa hanging over the latch. He could hear groaning sounds coming from inside. Hesitating and with trembling fingers, he unhooked the burqa, removed the key from the holder and opened the lock. Slowly and apprehensively, he pushed the door open. He stepped inside carefully and almost froze when he saw his boss lying on his stomach on the floor in a thick pool of his own blood. A broken flowerpot lay scattered all around him. In a state of utter shock and dismay, he bent down and tried to turn the unconscious SHO on his side but fell back when he saw the nib sticking out of his left eye. The barbarity of the act stunned him. He covered his mouth with his hands and let out a blood-curdling scream. But he knew he didn't have time to mourn; he had to act fast. He stood up and ran helter-skelter till he located the jeep keys. With great effort, he dragged the SHO outside, leaving a trail of blood and dirt, and managed to lay him on the back seat. He was shaking from the effort. He looked at his senior's face again; the pen was still in his eye. Without giving it another thought, he pulled it out and immediately covered the eye with a piece of cloth. Fortunately, this stopped the bleeding. He quickly took charge of the steering wheel and drove cautiously to the nearest hospital in Sadali district.

In the meantime, Bibi reached home to find a large group of women assembled in front of her home. They were surprised to see her without her burqa. As the tonga stopped, she stepped down, and, without saying a word to the women, rushed into her home and bolted the door from inside. But like jungle fire, stories about her act of bravery reached every ear in no time. It generated praise and fear in equal measure. Even though Sakhiullah was respected by the villagers, most women feared police retaliation. They were all aware of the brutality with which cops often operated, especially in rural areas where they were treated like demigods. When Sakhiullah arrived that evening, he was shocked to learn about the turn of events. He rushed to the army camp situated near his house and narrated the story to the deputy camp commander, a young army captain named Ishtiaq, who was also his first cousin. 'I need urgent help, Ishtiaq. We have no time to waste. It won't be long before the police come banging at our doors. And that could mean serious trouble; not only for Bibi, but for the entire family!'

The young captain nodded and called his most senior and experienced jawan at the camp, Subedar Major Mushtaq Khan, for advice. A deep furrow appeared between his brows as Sakhiullah related the story. He mused for a moment and then said, 'Sir, the camp commandant will have to intervene immediately as this is a case of attack on a serving police officer. But he's in Islamabad for the entire week. I know the SHO well. He's politically connected, highly corrupt and most brutal. If he survives, he will take revenge in every possible manner. But even if he doesn't, his colleagues won't spare your family. I suggest that you move out with your family immediately. Also, Bibi will have to be sent to India right away if we are to save her.'

Captain Ishtiaq looked at Sakhiullah and said, 'Bhaijaan, if what Mushtaq Sahib is saying is right, then we don't have much time. Please decide. I don't even have the authority to do what we are planning, but I shall not spare any effort.'

A helpless and confused Sakhiullah nodded in affirmation and the subedar swung into action.

An hour later, two military jeeps arrived at Sakhiullah's residence. Four army jawans in battle rig and armed with rifles stepped out, followed by a subedar and a young lieutenant. The lieutenant took Bibi into custody while Sakhiullah watched from a distance as a mute spectator. The military officer whispered in her ear that her life and that of her entire family was in danger. He explained to her that the arrest was being made only to evade a counter-attack as the police would not interfere with the military forces.

The first jeep left, taking Bibi to an unknown destination. Shortly, Sakhiullah too departed under escort. He was accompanied by his two minor sons and his cousin, Captain Ishtiaq. After travelling for about twenty kilometres, the first vehicle turned left from the narrow highway towards the Indian border while the second one turned right towards the main city. Bibi instinctively realized the plan. She cried and begged for an opportunity to meet her husband and children one last time. But her wails fell on deaf ears. Despite being aware of Sakhiullah's clout, the young army lieutenant displayed no mercy. He could not have; he was under strict instructions. The jeep reached the border half an hour later. The officer stepped down and went across the border, exchanged pleasantries with his counterpart from India and swiftly handed Bibi over to the Indian armed forces.

All by herself, in a land she had never seen before and amongst rank strangers, Bibi stood bewildered and scared.

An endless fence of thick barbed wire ran on either side of the barrier, which was manned by military forces. The Pakistani jeep was allowed to enter and return from the Indian side of the border because a Pakistani woman of Indian origin was involved. Not too far away stood an army truck filled with many more women who had been brought to the Indian side under similar circumstances. Most were unhappy. Many were crying inconsolably. They too were helped to disembark one by one and stand in a corner. Their plight was similar to that of Bibi. They had been uprooted and evicted against their will and thrown out of their homes just because their respective leaders had, without any application of mind, signed a treaty to send women back to their parents' homes just to earn brownie points. Family members of a few women had come to receive them, but the majority found themselves in no man's land and possibly discarded by either side. A few children, mostly girls, had also accompanied their mothers which showed the mindset of their families. Brutally battered, bruised, abused and without a home, the vulnerable women were faced with a bleak future in a land which was to be their new home but without the security umbrella of their kith and kin.

Bibi didn't know where to go. Her family in erstwhile India had been killed and her home destroyed. Her family in Pakistan was now behind her. The only saving grace was that the Indian soldiers were gentle and polite. They served the women meals on time and did everything in their control to make them comfortable. Simultaneously, they filled registers with data and contact details, and advised the women individually on the future course of action. It was a tedious task, but performed with great compassion and care by the Indian Army personnel.

Lance Naik Bharat Kumar was assigned to Bibi. He sat with her and heard her painful story with great patience, jotting down details for his reference later. Bibi's encounter with the SHO especially shocked him. He stopped writing and looked up at her petite frame, her slim fingers and innocent eyes, and mentally compared her with the ruffian. It did not make any sense! How could she have? Yet, the Pakistani lieutenant who had escorted her till the border had categorically mentioned her counter-attack as the main reason for her being deported. 'Her life is in danger,' he had said before leaving.

Bharat Kumar stood up from the chair, bowed in deep respect and took her permission to brief his boss. Half an hour later, he walked back from the administrator's office with the latter in tow. Major Samarth Singh Virk stepped inside the large refugee tent and saw Bibi sitting on a folding chair. He stood smartly to attention. Touched by the army officer's gesture, Bibi tried to get up. The major took a small step forward and gestured Bibi to be seated.

The soldier accompanying him hurriedly straightened up another folding chair. Major Virk took the seat and gently turned it to face Bibi, and what he saw was enough to mesmerize him. Despite her horrendous story, she looked like an angel who had fought hard to free herself from the clutches of a demon. He was having a hard time imagining that she had actually done what had been claimed. Nevertheless, he did not want to be caught staring at her, so he lowered his gaze. His gesture didn't go unnoticed and put Bibi at ease.

'Ma'am . . .' he began in a soft, polite tone, 'I know how you fought back and taught a lesson to the SHO at Sadali. Honestly, it sounds unbelievable. The cop is nothing but a wild beast. In comparison, you're a petite and simple mother of two young children. It is difficult to imagine that you put a brutal, heavyweight cop out of action for good, and that too with your bare hands.' The major paused before continuing. 'But the manner in which you were hurriedly brought here, under an army escort in a military jeep, without necessary documents, shows that you have definitely stepped on some heavy toes. Besides, one has heard of Balwant Singh and his gracious nobility. I want you to know that it's my honour and privilege to be of some service to you. We shall make all arrangements to ensure that you're suitably accommodated in a place of your choice.' Major Virk paused and looked at Bibi for a reaction and found her overwhelmed. Hearing her father's name, she began weeping.

Virk offered her a glass of water and continued. 'I wouldn't wish the level of mental and physical torture you've gone through even on an enemy. As of now, Pakistan is unsafe territory for you and for every non-Muslim. Besides, you are already on their radar for attacking a senior cop in uniform. They must be looking hammer and tongs for you and your husband. Hence, it was a wise decision by your husband and his cousin to shift you to India. Let's exercise patience, even though it's difficult for a mother to be away from her young children, and wait for new developments. I will do my best to get in touch with my contacts across the border and get updates at regular intervals.' Virk paused because she was still sobbing. But there was a hint of appreciation on her tearful face. He looked at the lance naik who immediately placed a table between the two. The major unfolded a map and circled a spot before continuing with his monologue.

'Ma'am, this village here called Tunda on the Indian side of Kashmir is closest to where you last stayed in Pakistan. It's inhabited by a healthy mix of fine people such as Kashmiri Pandits, Muslims, Sikhs and has a few Ladakhi families too. If you agree, we will make arrangements for your stay here. Effectively, it would be closest to your home in Pakistan Occupied Kashmir.

Hopefully, you'll be able to establish a channel and communicate with your family across the border. Who knows what the future has in store for you? But with this arrangement, we are hoping to establish communication with your loved ones. By the grace of the Almighty, you might be able to reunite with them in the near future.'

Bibi glanced at the map but couldn't figure out anything except black lines drawn in a zigzag pattern on a large green sheet. Virk understood her predicament. He pushed the map aside, prompting the alert lance naik to grab it midway. 'I suggest that you rest here at the military camp for a couple of days. I shall drive you to the village and show you around. If you want, we could also show you a few houses vacated by people who shifted to Pakistan.' Major Virk paused to see her reaction.

Left with no other choice, Bibi nodded and shut her eyes. Drop by drop, tears rolled down her pink cheeks. She was helpless, vulnerable, but by the grace of God there was help and she was safe even amongst strangers. Virk stood up. The sound of movement made Bibi open her eyes. The major took a step back and saluted again. 'We will make arrangements for your stay. Lance Naik Bharat Kumar will be here at your service if you need anything. And I live just a short distance away. You are absolutely safe. We will visit Tunda village day after tomorrow.'

Bibi managed to nod in agreement.

As soon as the major left the tent, she leaned back and shut her eyes. Scenes from her fight with the SHO flashed through her mind. She visualized her right hand grabbing the pen and lodging the one-inch-long metallic nib into his eye with all her strength. The more she tried to divert her mind from the violent act she was party to, the more it haunted her. Scenes of her kicking the SHO in his groin, adding insult to his injuries, kept coming back. *From where did I get such courage?* she wondered. Then her thoughts shifted to her family. The fact that she had been separated from her children in just a few hours pained her immensely. She opened her eyes with a sudden jerk of her head. She looked around and realized that she was in safe territory.

Standing at a short distance, the lance naik observed her closely but didn't move. *Time is the best healer,* he told himself. A short while later, two jawans entered the tent. They walked up to the lance naik and murmured something in his ear. He nodded in return and stepped closer to Bibi. 'Ma'am, your accommodation is ready. If you'll please follow us.' Wiping her eyes gently with her off-white cotton dupatta, she stood up and followed them towards the exit. Her feet unknowingly stamped the black burqa that had fallen from her lap. The two jawans stood to attention.

One of them tried to pick up the garment but the other jawan stopped his colleague. 'She won't need this any more . . .'

As Bibi walked past them, their eyes filled with deep admiration, respect and awe. It was clear that the story of her act of bravery had spread across the camp.

Perhaps they had begun treating her like one of them—a warrior and a protector.

5

Two days later, Bibi stepped out of her tent early in the morning to find a jawan waiting with a cup of tea on a wooden tray. 'Jai Hind, Memsahib,' he said as he stood to attention. Bibi accepted the tea hesitantly, mouthing, 'Jai Hind'. The words were not new to her. She had grown up with them and had heard them enough times at her parents' home. The same words had echoed in the Valley during the freedom struggle. Thousands of people had come on to the streets, mohallas and marketplaces and chanted them, shaking the very foundation of the British Raj. It had pushed the British forces into the safety of their barracks and forced the leadership to plan countermeasures. The Englishmen were masters of divide and rule, and had played the religion card to perfection. The Hindu–Muslim divide had worked and, to a great extent, had diluted the potency of the 'Jai Hind' slogan. The seeds of hatred sowed then had taken deep roots; its offshoots had yielded mistrust and turned great friends into arch-enemies. Bibi looked up at the blue, cloudless sky. There were no boundaries of caste or religion up there, no senseless bloodshed—it was all so peaceful, serene, vast and endless . . .

The nights were not kind to her. Her thoughts invariably went to her husband and children as soon as she put her head on the pillow. She missed them and worried about them, but there was no one with whom she could share her pain. Sakhiullah was unlike most others around him. He valued humanity, was kind and gentle and didn't care about what the world had to say. She was sure that he was capable of looking after their sons, but they were too young. She was still breastfeeding her younger son, and now the mother in her felt incomplete, tormented and devastated. Every night her breasts were engorged with milk, adding to the pain of her having to abandon her young, innocent and dependent children. The mere thought of them crying for her milk stirred her. Her heart was in intense turmoil; her soul cried and yearned to hold them in a tight embrace. Her feet itched and her hands trembled. She prayed fervently to God to keep her family safe. And finally, exhausted, she cried herself to a fitful sleep.

The morning brought some solace as there was activity around her and therefore some distraction—also the hope that she might get some news of her family or she might be able to reach out to them. Deep in thought, she sipped her tea, but the level in the cup didn't seem to go down. Tears continued to fall in a steady stream, adding to the brew. The jawan standing in front had been watching her and found it difficult to control his emotions. Mustering courage, he said, 'Memsahib, we are all praying that you reunite with your family. Please have faith.'

As if jolted from a deep slumber, Bibi opened her eyes and looked at him. She gave him a slight nod to acknowledge his sympathy. Her cheeks were flushed and there were shadows under her eyes. Her gaze shifted and fell on Major Virk who was walking in her direction. She placed the mug on the tray and got up to meet him midway. She greeted him with folded hands. 'Good morning, Ma'am, hope you slept well,' he said in response.

Bibi nodded gently and smiled but her face gave away her plight. She looked away nervously, scared that his gaze would open the floodgate of her emotions. The major was quick to notice and empathized with the situation she was in. Without making it obvious, he stopped a few feet away and briefly paused before beginning the discussion.

'I was wondering if we could leave for Tunda in an hour so that you get ample time to go around the village? I have served in this part of the Valley for the past two years and have found the villagers to be very innocent, humble, lovable and friendly. Post Partition, a few Kashmiris shifted to the other side of the border to be united with their loved ones. Their houses are still lying vacant. I would like you to take a look at the place. And if it suits you, we could help you settle down there.'

Bibi nodded but avoided making eye contact.

'All right then, I will come to pick you up at the right time. And here's a shawl for you, Ma'am. It's not the best, I am afraid, but it will give you adequate warmth.' Without waiting for Bibi's response, Major Virk saluted and turned to walk away.

Even though Bibi was quite used to the cold, she was in dire need of warm clothes and immediately wrapped it around her. The shawl felt good—as if someone had embraced and comforted her. She was with people she could trust.

Exactly an hour later, Major Virk arrived in his jeep followed by two escort vehicles. He was behind the wheel, dressed in a starched military uniform. An adjutant, a young lieutenant, sat on his left. He stepped out, saluted and opened the rear door. The men in the other vehicles too disembarked in a hurry and stood to attention. As soon as Bibi settled in, the men got into their respective vehicles and drove in the direction of Tunda.

The entire Valley was lush green. Birds were chirping a variety of songs, flowers were blooming and the sun was shining brightly on the horizon, spreading its warmth on the earth below. All through the hour-long drive, Bibi kept looking at the scenery around. It wasn't different from where she had come from, yet it was. Peace seemed to reign supreme, untouched by the tragedy that had befallen so many just across the border. As the jeep sped towards the destination, the road curving under its heavy wheels, Bibi sighed. She didn't know what destiny had in store for her, and she had no choice but to accept it.

As the olive-green military vehicles entered Tunda, Virk slowed down so that Bibi could take a closer look at the village life. He stopped the jeep at the small marketplace in the heart of the village. Shopkeepers rushed towards the vehicles, their faces radiant with joy. Bibi stepped out and looked around. Her expression changed when her eyes landed on a building at the far end. She suddenly grew excited. Virk noticed the sudden change in her mood, but before he could react, Bibi rushed to the nearest shopkeeper and pointed at a flagpole wrapped in an orange cloth. 'Is that a gurdwara?' she asked eagerly.

Without looking up to see in which direction she was pointing, the shopkeeper replied, 'Yes. It is. If you like, my son, Kumar, can escort you there.'

Bibi's face lit up with joy. Folding her hands together, she pleaded, 'Oh, that would be great!' Virk overheard the conversation and came rushing in. Bibi looked at him with questioning eyes. 'I want to visit the gurdwara. Do I have your permission, Sir?' Her softly uttered words in English both surprised and disturbed Major Virk. He understood the impact of what Bibi had gone through, the intensity of the violence she had witnessed.

Recovering quickly, he said, 'Of course, Ma'am. It is your right. You are in Hindustan now. You don't need anyone's permission to pray to God, any God.' He watched her, fascinated, as the look on her face changed from that of a grieving mother to childlike wonder.

'Oh, thanks so much! I am sorry, Sir, it's all so sudden.' He laughed and nodded.

The shopkeeper's son came out of the shop and escorted her to the gurdwara. Major Virk watched her walk away at a brisk pace as if she had an appointment with the lord. The young lieutenant came and stood next to the major. Virk placed his hand on his shoulders and said, 'She's deeply shattered, so much that it's going to be an acid test even for her God. She thinks that by merely bowing inside the gurdwara her problems would be solved. She doesn't understand how the politics of religion have wrecked her life. I pray that her wishes come true, but I'm worried that things might not be as easy . . .'

The young officer nodded in agreement. 'Ameen,' he said, his eyes shut momentarily in prayer.

A little while later, Bibi returned to where they were standing, followed by the little boy, Kumar. She was visibly calmer. *Perhaps she did get to meet her God after all*, wondered the major. Bibi thanked the shopkeeper and gently patted the boy on his head. And then, turning towards Major Virk, she said, 'I would like to stay in this village. Can we look at the available houses?'

Virk smiled in return, nodded gently and said to himself, *It's so important to have faith. Why am I not surprised?*

The adjutant, Lieutenant Pankaj Bhardwaj, took the lead and escorted Bibi to one of the first shortlisted houses close to the market. Its ground floor was occupied by an aged couple—Allah Rakha and his wife Begum Shahida—who had been told about the visit. The couple was working in their kitchen garden, and seeing Virk and his team heading towards them, they stepped forward and greeted the visitors. Virk bowed in return with folded hands. After exchanging pleasantries, Virk said, 'Khan Sahib, as we had discussed, this lady here would like to take a look at the first floor of the house. Please show her the place. She has been separated from her family across the border and desperately needs the support and company of noble people. I would be grateful if you could help.'

Allah Rakha responded immediately, 'Why not, with pleasure.' He then turned towards Bibi and said politely,

'You're most welcome to stay with us like a part of our family. Please follow me.' He bowed, took a step back and turned towards the dark-green staircase. Despite his age, the alacrity with which he moved surprised Bibi. She followed him up the wooden stairs that led to the first-floor entrance. There was a bounce in her young feet. About ten minutes later, she came back by the same route. The old wooden structure creaked under her feet. She waited a moment for the old man to come down, bowed a respectful farewell to him and then walked up to where Major Virk was standing. Her eyes were no longer moist. There were signs of hope in her body language, energy in her stride and traces of impatience in her conversation. Without exchanging any words with Virk, she smiled at the jawan who was holding the vehicle door for her and sat inside the jeep. Virk remained quiet which allowed Bibi to regain her composure and re-evaluate her decision. A good half an hour into the journey, Bibi spoke. Her voice was calm and controlled, and she appeared happy. 'When can I shift here, Sir?'

6

Days turned into months, but the distance between Pakistan and India only widened with each passing moment. Nothing happened for Bibi except that she found herself adjusting to a new life and surroundings. Her presence, though, created quite a stir in the small village. Stories of her beauty spread far and wide. And because she was alone and vulnerable, she became an easy target for the local ruffians who began eyeing her and following her on her trips to the gurdwara. They did not bother her though, because they were aware that she enjoyed military protection. She lived peacefully for the first six months.

One day, on one of his visits to the village, Major Virk informed her that his *pultan* was moving to Rajasthan. 'Ma'am, I shall stay in touch but orders are orders.' Bibi nodded, deeply saddened as she had begun to rely on him. Virk continued, 'I have also received credible information that your husband and children are safe. They have shifted to an unknown destination to stay safe from the cops. They're somewhere near Hassan Abdal.' Tears sprung from her eyes at the mention of her family, and she quickly lowered her head. Virk noticed but didn't make any move to placate her. Instead, he continued with what he had come to tell her. 'There is something else too. The SHO was suitably punished for his act. He's become permanently blind in one eye. Post the incident, he became bedridden for a long time and eventually lost sensation in his right leg. As a result, he was discharged from the police force.' Virk paused, a little unsure of what he was about to say next.

'Please continue. Don't hide anything from me. I have seen enough in my short life to accept everything with grace,' she said politely.

'Your husband has married again,' Virk replied.

Bibi heard him but didn't react. Her worries began surfacing again, making her restless and anguished. One by one, the pillars of hope she had built fell apart. She was worried about the future of her children who were now dependent on their stepmother. Would she take care of them like Bibi had? Now that so much time had passed, did her children still remember her?

Her own safety was shrouded in uncertainty now. Virk's occasional visits to Tunda had acted like a protective umbrella. She was aware that her beauty and singlehood were drawing undue attention. In comparison to the burqa she wore in Tadali, which protected her from undue exposure, her dupatta enhanced her beauty manifold. Allah Rakha and his wife often lovingly compared her headscarf to the dark clouds through which her bright and beautiful face emerged like the full moon. Till now, no one had dared to harass her, or even pass a rude comment. Major Virk's presence was comforting. Since he was loved and feared in equal proportions in the district, his reference itself was a passport to safety from prying eyes. His departure, she feared, could spell trouble for her.

Virk too sensed that she was insecure, but he was helpless. He knew he had no control over the situation from hundreds of miles away. After his chat with Bibi and a cup of Kashmiri kehwa, he departed. In a matter of weeks, everyone in the village became aware of his pultan's plan to move to the deserts. For the local goon, Ismail, this meant freedom. He and his friends soon began loitering around Bibi's home. With every passing day, they became more confident; they were also encouraged by the fear-filled silence of the neighbours. They closely monitored her movements and followed her during her daily visits to the gurdwara. The villagers feared Ismail and were not bold enough to even look him in the eye. With Major Virk out of the way, he boldly told his gang members about his plan of 'taming' Bibi and began looking for an opportunity to 'prove' his manliness.

He did not have to wait long.

It was one of those days when the sky was overcast with heavy clouds. Winter had set in early that year, forcing the villagers to stay in the comfort of their warm homes. Bibi had finished her daily chores later than usual and, as a result, by the time she finished her prayers at the gurdwara, the sun was already setting behind the mountains. Walking all alone on the dark, lonely stretch, she was spotted by the ever alert Ismail. With his face and head wrapped tightly in a muffler, he started following her but remained on the other side of the road lest she recognize him.

He waited for her to start climbing the stairs to her house and then rushed towards her, climbing two steps at a time, and put his foot in the door before Bibi could shut it. Then he entered her house forcibly and bolted the door from inside. He put his hand over her mouth and dragged her towards the bedroom. A helpless Bibi made a valiant effort to free herself, but failed against his powerful grip. She tried to bite his hand but her teeth couldn't make an impact. Despite her petite figure and matching body weight, her stiff resistance surprised the bully. Initially, he smiled and took it as a challenge, but her continued struggle began to annoy him. He soon lost his patience. He turned her face towards him and swung his right hand with full force. His palm struck Bibi's left cheek. She fell on the chair to her right and began bleeding profusely. The impact of the slap was so strong that she lost consciousness momentarily.

Sensing victory, Ismail began to relax and bent down to take a closer look at her, hurling abuses while doing so. He ripped open her woollen pheran and threw it aside. And then, grabbing her hands, dragged her into the bedroom. Once inside, he picked her up effortlessly and put her on the bed. Smiling to himself, he went towards the fireplace and lit up the dry wood. He rubbed his hands gently and then began removing his thick woollen sweater. As his arms went up, holding the two sides of the garment and pulling it over his face, he felt a sharp metallic object entering the right side of his back. He doubled up in pain and then tripped and fell. But before he could steady himself, Bibi thrust the sharp metal farther into his back. He fell down with a thud. The six-inch-long kitchen knife stayed embedded in his spine. Letting go of the sweater hanging over his head, his hands reached out to the wound. His eyes were covered by the thick garment and he was unable to see anything. In the meantime, Bibi bent down and quickly grabbed one of the burning wooden logs from the fireplace.

Like a wounded tigress, she jumped over his body. Her own nose was bleeding. But equally red were her eyes, spitting fire. She was ready to wreak vengeance on him. She raised the burning log over her head and then, with all her strength, thrust it into Ismail's face. The woollen sweater immediately caught fire and burnt his face. Screaming in pain and rubbing his eyes, Ismail pushed her off and rushed to the small balcony. The fire had engulfed his face and was rapidly spreading to his chest and back.

Writhing in pain and bleeding profusely, Ismail struggled to unlatch the door leading to the balcony. He somehow managed to open it and leapt off from the guard rail, falling with a loud thud. Bibi followed him. The log in her hand was still aglow with embers and so were her eyes, matching the very shade of crimson. She saw Ismail lying head down on the concrete floor, crying in pain, bleeding and screaming out loud for help. The Valley reverberated with his sharp, blood-curdling shrieks.

Then suddenly, as if on cue, dozens of houses lit up one by one. Scores of lanterns came alive. Windows were flung open and inquisitive heads popped out. But no door opened. No one came out. Seeing the tiny dots of light, Ismail's wails grew louder. But nothing happened. His cries went unanswered. The burning wicks flickered at first and then went out almost as suddenly as they had come on, engulfing the Valley in darkness once again. The villagers had identified the man but were not willing to help him. Standing on the balcony, Bibi witnessed the Valley plunge into darkness. She was about to turn towards her room when she heard the sound of Allah Rakha's front door creaking. He stepped out and pushed his foot beneath the goon's half-burnt face to check his injuries. Ismail screamed out aloud again and begged for help. The kitchen knife was still embedded in his back.

Taking a step back, Allah Rakha looked up and waved his hands, motioning Bibi to go inside. She obeyed but not quite. She stood behind the half-closed door and watched the action under way. She saw Allah Rakha pulling Ismail by his arms. He dragged his body across the dusty, dark road and then pushed him down the valley. Alive. The heavy body rolled down the steep hill till it hit the sharp rocks. His one last painful cry reverberated across the valley. But this time, no oil lamp lit up and no window opened.

Shocked, Bibi forgot her own pain and hurriedly cupped her mouth with her palms. An eerie silence descended soon after, pierced only by the sounds of the night. A few minutes later, Shahida too reached the spot and stood next to her husband. She had a long broom in her hand. Allah Rakha took it from her and began sweeping the debris and burnt pieces of wool. Shahida joined him. Satisfied with their work, the aged couple walked back towards their home. Before entering, they looked up to check if Bibi's door was closed. Contented, they went inside their house and shut the door. Bibi stood in silence till she heard the sound of Allah Rakha's door bolting. Even in her wildest dreams, she had not anticipated such a turn of events. It dawned on her that she had turned two innocent, lovable and pious humans into murderers. She rushed into the kitchen, washed her face with cold water and began crying bitterly. *Why did I do this? Why did I not kill myself instead? O God, please help me. This is not the karma I wished to perform!* Then she thought about her loneliness, her family and cried some more. *A bird that is born in a cage often thinks that freedom is a crime.*

About ten minutes later, Bibi heard a gentle knock on her door. She ran into the kitchen, splashed water on her face, straightened her hair and went towards the main entrance. She unlocked the door to find Allah Rakha and Shahida. The latter was holding a bowl of warm water and a towel in her hands. Shahida spoke first. 'Now we know how you dealt with the Pakistani SHO. Though the cop survived, this goon met his fate. And hopefully, his accomplices will get the message and leave you alone,' she said in a firm, motherly tone and escorted Bibi inside. They made her sit and applied a home-made concoction on her wounds to relieve her of the pain.

It was hard for Bibi to believe that the fingers that were applying balm on her wounds belonged to the same hands that had tossed a fully-grown man into the valley alive a few minutes ago. Shahida broke her reverie by placing a gentle hand on her shoulder and giving her a glass of warm milk mixed with saffron and honey. As she took a sip of the liquid, she burst into tears.

'What happened?' inquired a worried Shahida.

'Your love and care reminded me of the man who adopted me, Syed Baba. I don't know why the lord is toying with a shattered earthen pot like me,' Bibi replied between sobs. Shahida patted her forehead and helped her lie down on the bed. Allah Rakha settled down on the wooden floor next to the bed. Before going to sleep, he said, 'In a bookshop, both Gita and Quran sit next to each other. They never quarrel. The ones who fight in their names are those who have never read them . . .'

After the women had drifted off to sleep, the old man quietly exited the room and closed the door gently behind him. He cleaned up the blood spots on the floor, rearranged the kitchen and went back to his apartment. The next morning, he went back to Bibi's house again. But before he could knock, Shahida opened the door and signalled him to remain quiet. 'She's sound asleep, let her rest,' she whispered. 'Once she's awake, let's all go to the gurdwara. She will find solace there,' she said. Allah Rakha nodded in agreement and returned to his house. Shahida sat down on the floor and began praying. With tears in her eyes and a prayer on her lips, she said, 'If you're there, Allah, and listening, then please don't test my child any more. Send her a good husband. She needs to live the beautiful life that you've blessed her with. Thank you.'

7

These two incidents—one in Pakistan and one in India—had shaken Bibi. They had both resulted in violence and gore. One day, she sat in her prayer posture, with her legs folded beneath her, her eyes closed and her palms on her knees, and analysed her actions in minute detail. It was difficult for her to fathom what had transformed her from a quiet, god-fearing woman into a savage beast in a flash. In the case of the SHO, she had continued to attack him even after blinding him in one eye, nearly killing him in the process. On both occasions, in a fit of anger, her mind had let her animal instinct take over her rationality. The sudden rush of blood in her veins had miraculously made her lift the heavy flowerpot with ease and smash it with full force on his sensitive parts. Something similar had happened with Ismail where she had set him on fire even after stabbing him.

She was surprised and disturbed to realize that deep within, her subconscious mind was not troubled by the far-reaching consequences of her actions. On the contrary, she felt vindicated. Seeing her attackers lying helplessly on the ground, begging for help, had made her sigh with satisfaction. There was no fear in her heart or mind. She was, as if possessed by a demon, out to settle all scores.

Her eyes jerked open; they were filled with fear of what she had become in those moments. She touched her forehead with her hand to find tiny sweat drops. She wiped her face and gulped down a glass of water. But the uneasiness refused to go away. She somehow managed to close her eyes again. Was it all related to the bloodshed she had witnessed as a child? Had she kept the violence within her and it had erupted when she had felt cornered? She stood up and rushed to the kitchen. But the cold-water splashes on her face made little difference in getting rid of the feelings of shock and guilt. Instead, her mind went back to Ismail and his gory death.

After stabbing the goon twice with a sharp kitchen knife kept by her bedside, she still had the strong urge to burn him alive. She had placed the knife under her pillow, fearing such an incident would occur. It became increasingly difficult for her to understand what evil possessed her and made her change into a wild, bloodthirsty beast. She had witnessed Allah Rakha drag Ismail to the edge of the cliff and push him to his death and still had made no effort to stop him. Instead, she had felt at ease, relieved.

Was it her instinct that had made her act like this or was violence a part of her? She didn't have an answer, nor did she know whom to consult for guidance. Her mother had taught her about the essence of love and patience. Her father had inculcated values of sharing and caring. And here she was, turning into a vicious attacker, a murderer. Her heart ached. Her soul was burdened. She repented her actions and feared seeing her own reflection in the mirror. Still, she wasn't sure she wouldn't do it again.

While returning from the gurdwara a week later, she saw Pandit Kishan Kaul entering his home. She waved at him. A few minutes later, she was seated on his carpeted floor, talking to the saintly soul. Mustering all her courage, she told him her story and the state of her mind. At first, he was quite shaken. He had heard the stories about her, but, barring a small percentage, had discounted most of them. But when he heard it directly from Bibi, it made him feel both proud and concerned.

He remained silent for some time, then abruptly stood up and went inside his room. A minute later, he emerged with two glasses of water. Offering one to Bibi, he gulped down the other, took a deep breath and began, 'I am quite touched and shaken by your journey so far. Deep inside, you are nursing serious injuries. Your mind and heart are unable to let go of the violence, bloodshed, the immeasurable pain and hurt suffered by you and your family. Thus this revolt within. But your soul is intact. These tears of repentance are a sign that you wish to return to the path of nobility.'

He paused, looked at her closely and continued, 'Please remember, even the best of world conquerors ultimately realized that hate wasn't the solution to their problems or success. Even though most of their desires were fulfilled by acts of war, yet they didn't carry anything home. Except for our karma, we will go exactly the way we arrived when we were born, empty-handed. We reap what we sow. This is the basic law of nature. No one, howsoever big, can get away from this simple truth.' Pandit Kaul stopped briefly, drank whatever little water was remaining in the glass and explained further, 'I am not surprised that you survived two vicious attacks by taking on forces far more strong than you. Lord Krishna said, "If you don't fight for what you want, then don't cry for what you've lost." Life itself is a series of tiny miracles. The lord makes a way when there seems to be none. On both these occasions, you were being attacked. You received help when you were helpless, defenceless, but willing to fight back. The fact that you have compassion even for people like the SHO and Ismail shows that you have forgiven them. That in itself is a blessing. The darkest hour of the night is the first indication of the bright sunshine ahead. I think you should look inwards and meditate. Each one of us has a separate path. And it appears to me that you will see yours very soon because of your desire to travel on one.'

The water-filled copper tumbler was still next to her, but her thirst had been quenched. She had found answers to her queries. She stood up, bowed and said, 'Thank you, Panditji, your sermons have worked like magic, done wonders to my psyche. I am so grateful.' She took her leave and made her way back to her house. She was already feeling better. There was renewed energy in her stride. She went straight to her bedroom and lifted the pillow. Underneath it, wrapped in a plain white cloth, was the kitchen knife. It again reminded her of all the atrocities life had thrown at her. She picked it up, dropped it in a waste bin and washed her hands clean. She felt happy. She was free from fear and violence. Bowing gently in front of the picture of her deity, she sought forgiveness and said, 'Dear Lord, I cannot be violent and spiritual at the same time. I surrender to you. Please help me undertake this new journey and assist me in reaching my destination.'

About a month after Ismail's death, the local police came knocking. They had found the badly decomposed body of a man whom they suspected was Ismail. Even though Bibi had been given a clean chit by the village head, the inspector decided to meet her and complete the paper formalities as her name had come up during his inquiries. He was dressed in civil clothes and was accompanied by her neighbour, Allah Rakha Khan. The meeting took place at Bibi's residence. Inspector Jung Bahadur had heard of her beauty but was bowled over when he met her face-to-face.

Bibi's very first answer to his question, however, took him by surprise. 'Did you know Ismail?' the cop asked. In response, Bibi nodded in affirmation and then went on to elaborate, much to the chagrin of Allah Rakha.

'Yes, I knew him. He tried to molest me. I retaliated, attacked him with a kitchen knife and nearly burnt him with firewood. He was injured and jumped out of the balcony.' Bibi deliberately stopped midway but didn't lower her gaze. A visibly shocked Jung Bahadur began scratching his head. Given his vast experience, he was able to instantly build the scene and how it must have unfolded. There was honesty in her eyes, and he knew she was telling the truth.

Allah Rakha, shell-shocked by what he had just heard, interrupted and went on to give a different version of the incident. 'Sir, Ismail was a known criminal. When he attacked Bibi and tried to molest her, we immediately learnt about it. These wooden roofs aren't soundproof, you see. I rushed up and began banging on the front door. Ismail panicked and jumped from the balcony. Sadly, he fell on the concrete and got badly injured. We treat Bibi as our own daughter. Out of anger and vengeance, I dragged his body across the road and threw him off the cliff. Therefore, I am responsible for Ismail's death and not Bibi.' Allah Rakha drove his point home by banging a tumbler repeatedly on the table.

Jung Bahadur sighed and closed his case diary. 'Baba,' he began softly. 'All my life I have dealt with criminals. Ismail was a history-sheeter. He attacked Bibi and she reacted in self-defence. However, and more importantly, the police are not even sure the body is Ismail's. What if he returns tomorrow? Two innocent, law-abiding citizens cannot be punished for defending themselves from an attack. I very much appreciate your honesty, but there's no proof, nor is there any sign of Ismail. I am therefore closing the case here and now. Both the country and our society need people like you. Please look after her. She has already suffered enough. May you all stay blessed. Thank you.'

As an afterthought, he asked Bibi, 'Ismail was a known gangster. Weren't you scared of the consequences while counter-attacking him?'

Bibi smiled and replied, 'Life has taught me that the giant in front of you is never bigger than the God within you.'

Inspector Bahadur stood up and walked towards the exit. Upon reaching the door, he stopped, turned slowly and returned to where Bibi was sitting. Seeing him coming back, she hurriedly stood up. Bahadur went closer, looked into her beautiful, calm eyes and spoke in a respectful tone. 'I admire you for your courage, Bibi. Even after facing unspeakable brutality, trauma and injustice, you are not scared to speak the truth, nor compromise your principles. Nor are you willing to tolerate injustice. It is a unique gift, bestowed upon the rarest, most special souls. It's obvious that you're being tested by God. I shall pray that you emerge with flying colours. May all your wishes come true.'

Then, without waiting for her response, the inspector placed his right hand over Bibi's head as a mark of blessing and left. Bibi couldn't help but compare the cop in her new home town in Kashmir with the one she had left behind in Pakistan. One had gone on merits and tried to impart justice after much deliberation, while the other had abused his power to satisfy his own lust, greed and ego. *Would it be possible for her family to shift to India?* She began thinking and hoping.

Like fire, the word about Ismail's death at Bibi's hands spread far and wide. It all began with one set of lips whispering the secret, and by evening the entire Valley was aware of Bibi's fight against the most dreaded criminal.

'How did she do it?' everyone wanted to know.

'She has supernatural powers,' said one of her immediate neighbours.

'Oh, she is no less than a goddess herself,' commented another.

The menfolk were especially taken aback. Ismail was a known criminal. Almost all the small makeshift shop owners had stories about how his gang would rob them. Now he was gone and they had only Bibi to thank. Even though nothing had been officially said, the inspector's visit to her house had confirmed it.

Unaware of the celebration in the Valley, Bibi went about her daily chores. However, on her way to the market, she noticed that the attitude of the women had changed towards her. They stopped, smiled and bowed. The men too wished her aloud with folded hands. Their tone was respectful and their eyes reflected gratitude.

Deeply perplexed, Bibi stopped at the shop she frequented and gave her handwritten list of daily items to the shopkeeper. He immediately grabbed the paper and said, 'Don't worry, Bibi. My son, Ahmed, will deliver these items to your house. Thank you.'

Overwhelmed by his effusiveness, she pulled out money from her purse and asked, 'That would be great, but please tell me, how much should I pay?' She'd barely finished her sentence when Zaira, the shopkeeper's wife, emerged from behind a curtain that separated the shop and the stockroom. She was not wearing her traditional burqa. Her beautiful face was radiant and her eyes were sparkling.

'Welcome to our shop, Bibi. We're grateful. Please don't embarrass us by offering money. You're a godsend. Allow us to do our bit. Please, I request you.'

Without getting into an argument, she left the shop and headed for home. Her mind was clouded. She didn't understand why she was being given special treatment. As soon as she reached her house, she opened the front gate and rushed up the staircase. Her hands trembled as she unlocked the door. The sound of footsteps on the stairs startled her. It was Ahmed, the shopkeeper's son. He was almost panting. 'Amma sent this,' he said as he handed her the bag of groceries. As soon as she took it, he turned back and rushed down the steps without asking for money.

Bibi entered her house, placed the bag on the table and stood in front of the photo frame on the wall with folded hands. 'Babaji, what's happening? Why are they behaving like this? What have I done? Please help me!'

Her prayers had barely left her lips, when Shahida walked in. Bibi ran and hugged her tightly. 'Why are they treating me like this, Ma? What have I done?'

Shahida patted her on her back gently and said, 'You have done what no one could do. You've got them freedom from Ismail. The girls, women and even men are feeling safe and secure now. I wanted to come and tell you that the womenfolk want to meet and thank you but before I

71

could, you had left for the bazaar. Just look outside your balcony. There are so many people waiting to meet you.'

Bibi rushed to her bedroom and flung open the balcony door. Shahida was right. A horde of women looked up at her. She buried her face in her hands and then rushed inside to hug Shahida again.

'Don't be afraid, my child. Allah chose you. Ismail got what he deserved. The village is grateful to you. Just accept this as a reward and forget everything else,' she concluded and gently pushed her towards the door.

As soon as Bibi climbed down the steps, the women came forward and stood around her. They then hugged her one by one. Most of them had tears in their eyes as if a major catastrophe had been averted and they were safe now. No one spoke about Ismail's death but said: 'Shukria, Bibi.' After a while, they all went back to their respective homes. But they left behind small gifts, souvenirs and flowers, neatly placed outside Shahida's door.

* * *

About eight months passed. Despite her best efforts, Bibi received no news about her family's whereabouts from Major Virk or other sources. But she never gave up hope. She did small jobs, stitched clothes and saved money. Her sole mission was to travel to Pakistan and search for her family. Her acts of bravado and daily service at the gurdwara had made her a known face in the area.

One day, while walking back home, she saw a jeep abruptly pulling over to the side. Bibi recognized the driver in his dark-green turban. She went closer and cheerfully greeted Virk. There was excitement and exuberance on her face as if she were meeting a long-lost friend. She observed that an additional star had been added to his uniform. 'You've lost weight, Sir,' she complimented. 'And you have forgotten us. Looks like responsibilities are weighing heavily on you.'

Virk was overjoyed to see her in good spirits even after what she had been through. Leaving the jeep behind with his driver, he began walking with her towards her home. He looked around at the shopkeepers and acknowledged their waving hands. 'It's so nice to be back,' he said as he stepped on to the freshly painted wooden stairs leading to Bibi's apartment. Once inside, he sat in the living room briefly and then followed her to the kitchen to find her preparing kehwa.

Bibi looked up at him and noticed that something was bothering him. But before she could ask, Virk spoke up. 'May I take a look at the balcony?' He waited for her response. She nodded.

Virk walked to the balcony door. He unbolted it and pushed it open. A gust of fresh wind hit him in the face. He stepped out and looked down to find Allah Rakha looking up at him. Standing close by was his wife, Shahida. He waved at them and exchanged pleasantries. Virk noticed the relief on their faces. His eyes scanned the road and the steep ridge beyond. Rubbing his beard gently, he turned back to find Bibi standing with two cups of steaming kehwa.

'Yes, that's where Ismail fell. But how did you come to know?'

Virk accepted the cup and took a long sip. He looked at her closely with immense admiration but didn't respond. Closing the door behind him, he walked towards the small living room and perched himself on the same chair. Bibi sat opposite him and placed her mug on the table. 'I am extremely grateful to you for bringing me here, Sir. I couldn't have withstood the trauma that I was carrying on my soul all by myself. This place and the beautiful people here have helped me overcome what at one point looked like an impossible past. I have been looking for an opportunity to convey my deep gratitude to you. Only I didn't know how to reach you.' Bibi spoke like she was delivering a well-rehearsed speech.

Virk smiled. *She has matured and is able to handle her emotions well,* he told himself. Bibi replenished his cup and went back into the kitchen. The sound of banging utensils told him that she was preparing a meal. That she didn't even ask him before cooking showed that she considered him someone she had a right on. It made him feel at home.

They ate in silence. Bibi instinctively knew that Virk had been promoted to the rank of lieutenant colonel, but he was not there to make a courtesy call or celebrate his promotion. There was something far more important that had made him drive all the way to Tunda, but he was taking time to open up. She did not inquire or push him to speak his mind.

Virk finished his meal and washed his hands. From his expression, she could make out that he had liked what he had eaten. Bibi brought in more kehwa, and they both filled their respective mugs. His silence was killing her. She finally decided to break the ice. 'Where are you posted now? And how long are you going to be here? Have you made any arrangements to stay or are you heading back to the district headquarters?' Her voice was filled with confidence, yet carried traces of concern and affection. Virk felt encouraged to speak his mind.

He put the mug down, placed his elbows on the table and looked at Bibi admiringly. Then, clearing his throat, he said, 'I have been getting a few reports regarding your welfare. I also learnt about this Ismail attack. But it was well after everything was over and the matter was closed by the police. The reports also stated that our relations with Pakistan won't improve any time soon. On the contrary, if at all, they are becoming worse. And I don't see the two nations putting their differences aside. It's therefore becoming more difficult to get an update on your family in Pakistan. I will continue to push, but we have little hope as my sources are drying up.' Virk paused again as if summoning up the courage to say what he actually wanted to. A moment later, he finally gave it away, 'Amrit, the real purpose of my coming here is to ask you something. Will you marry me?' After completing his sentence, he nervously waited for her response.

Bibi was stunned. This was the last thing she had expected to hear from a decorated army officer. She tightened her grip around the porcelain mug in excitement, her hands damp and clammy with sweat. She found it difficult to look into his eyes. She was a legally married woman with two children. And here she was, dining with a stranger, considering her own marriage proposal. Gathering some courage, she replied, 'How can I discuss a matter that is not in my control? You are aware of my marital status and my children. I don't quite understand all this.'

Virk responded instantly as if he was prepared for her questions. 'What happened in Pakistan was a forced compromise. The man who adopted you married you to his brother's son because that was the only way to protect you. You were a minor then, not in a position to say "no" even if you wanted to. You cannot go to Pakistan and they cannot come to India, not over the next few decades as I see it. And even if they do, or you manage to reach Pakistan, how will you find them? I have used all my resources but have not been able to go beyond Hassan Abdal in northern Pakistan. There's no trace of them. All we know is, given his position and wealth, he has moved on with his life. Either way, you cannot allow your life to drag on, hoping to get a glimpse of someone whom you cannot be with.' He fell silent and waited for her to speak.

She weighed her words and spoke softly. Her voice had traces of helplessness. 'But this is immoral. It's not acceptable in our society. What will people say? How will our society react?'

Virk replied, 'Given the circumstances under which your wedding was solemnized, it would be treated as null and void in any court of law. Living all by yourself, you're vulnerable and unsafe. You have been lucky in the past. God knows who else is lusting after you. I know it's too sudden, this proposal of mine, but I have been thinking about it for a long time.' Virk paused again, took another sip of the brew and continued. 'You should think about your own future and life. I don't want an answer right away. Discuss it with Allah Rakha Sahib and his wife. I will come back tomorrow. But you should know that I am not married, and we have an age difference of about ten years between us.' Virk stood up, bowed gently, turned and walked towards the door.

As he pulled the latch, Bibi called out, 'But Sir, you didn't tell me where you are staying.'

Virk looked at her, smiled and said, 'Oh, the army mess, about 50 kilometres from here.' By then, he had pulled open the door partially, allowing the cold breeze to fill the room. Her dupatta slipped from her head and rested on her shoulders. But she made no attempt to put it back. The toes of her pink bare feet were twitching, showing signs of nervousness. Those feet had suffered endless pain but had successfully carried her a long distance from Pakistan so that she could meet her true life partner.

'It's too far. Maybe you should stay here,' she uttered in a sweet, soft and hesitant voice.

Virk stopped in his tracks and looked at her closely. A gust of wind ruffled her hair which covered her eyes. But she made no attempt to comb it back. Her shy smile said everything that Virk wanted to hear. He shut the door, went closer and took her in his arms. Tears welled up in her eyes and began rolling down her cheeks. She held him tightly. Her eyes were shut. But deep within, she knew that she had found her soulmate. This was the first time in her life that she was holding a man with both her arms.

'Thank you, Lord,' she murmured to herself. 'I am grateful.'

Virk could hear her whisper.

'Thank you, Amrit,' he said loudly as he tightened his embrace, giving her the warmth and comfort she had been desperately looking for. Far away, the setting sun's golden hue was painting the Valley orange. Merged in it were two hearts, basking under the umbrella of new-found love.

8

The next morning, Bibi and Virk came down together to talk to Allah Rakha and Shahida. The aged couple was standing on the landing, smiling joyously and looking content. Bibi bent low and touched their feet. It was now Shahida's turn to get emotional. She looked at Virk and said, 'We were so anxious when you went up to her house yesterday. Till date, no one has dared to do that except one person who paid a huge price for it. But when you didn't come down, my heart said that my daughter has finally found a suitable match. We are so happy. Please come in, son. *Khushamdeed* [Welcome]!'

Virk entered first, followed by Bibi and the aged couple. Bibi went straight to the kitchen and began preparing kehwa. Shahida entered a few minutes later, and the two women hugged each other. 'At last our prayers have been answered. We feel so blessed that we will be able to see you off to your new home. What a fine gentleman he is. I am sure he will also prove to be a great husband. Now please go inside and sit with Abba. I will bring the tea.'

Bibi did as she was told and went out to the living room to find Virk in a deep and serious conversation with Allah Rakha. She sat next to the old man, diagonally opposite Virk, gazing at him lovingly. 'I have a request to make,' Allah Rakha said. 'We would like you to marry our daughter at the gurdwara in the presence of the entire village. We are too old to travel. Please accept our humble request.'

Virk looked at his shy bride-to-be and smiled in affirmation. 'I agree, Baba. But I have a small request too. I am here just for a week, and I want to take her along with me when I go. Can you help me with the wedding arrangements? I don't have enough time to call my parents, even though I know they would have been delighted to be a part of their only son's wedding.'

Allah Rakha responded instantly, 'Of course we can!'

'And we will!' added an excited Shahida as she emerged from the kitchen. 'But till then, you will stay on the first floor and Bibi with us.' A shy Bibi stood up to help Shahida with the tray she was holding. It was laden with bowls of dry fruit and empty tea mugs. Shahida went into the kitchen and came back with a copper kettle that had a long spout. Together, the two women served tea and snacks.

'I agree, Ammiji,' Virk responded. 'Thank you for the accommodation. It's quite helpful.'

Bibi looked up and gazed at Virk. Their eyes met. Bibi blushed and immediately looked away. Shahida giggled. Allah Rakha lifted his hands, thanking Allah. After a very long time, their home was filled with sounds of joy and happiness. Seeing her husband pray, Shahida's eyes filled up and she wiped them with the back of her hands. Their joy knew no bounds. Their prayers had been answered. Her wrinkled cheeks glowed with happiness.

Soon, the day of the wedding was upon them. Allah Rakha and Pandit Kishan Kaul reached the gurdwara early in the morning to oversee the preparations. Bibi and Virk walked in together at the scheduled time. She was dressed in a beautiful red lehnga and he in a heavily embroidered kurta pyjama. She was radiant. Her flawless skin gleamed and her almond-shaped eyes shone with happiness. In spite of the bridal fineries, the red bindi between her beautifully shaped brows stood out. Growing up, she had seen her mother wearing one. But she had never had the opportunity to do so herself. While getting ready a few hours ago, her hands had trembled as she had placed the thin brush on her forehead to make the dot, but the mirror in front had reflected her mother's smiling face. Her eyes had filled up as she thought of her family that should've been a part of the celebrations. Standing close by, Shahida had read her mind and, taking the brush out of her hand, had painted the round red dot. 'It's all destiny, my dear daughter, all destiny. Let it go. It's time to welcome a bright future. I am sure your mother is watching you dress up from up there and giving you a thousand blessings,' she had said, holding Bibi's hands in hers, reassuring her.

Bibi and Virk took their positions to walk around the holy book. The two elderly men, from different religions, stood like pillars and blessed the couple. Led by her husband, like a dutiful wife, she went around it four times, holding in her hands the long cloth that tied the two together, the other end of which was held by her husband. At the fourth round, as the two bowed before the holy Granth, the entire hall, filled to the brim with villagers, began showering the couple with flowers. There were tears of joy in everyone's eyes. They knew how important the occasion was for Bibi. They too had prayed for her.

As the two stepped out of the gurdwara, groups of young girls encircled them, dancing and singing the traditional Kashmiri *bidai* (farewell) folk song while the elders clapped in unison. Military vehicles stood lined up on the tarmac behind the decorated olive-green car. On cue, all the assembled uniformed personnel saluted the bride. The two made a powerful couple, much adored by those around them.

Bibi went up to Shahida and handed her the key to her first-floor home. 'I cannot thank you enough, Ammi,' she said. 'You never made me feel like a motherless child. Bless me so that I can start my own home and run it like you do, with utmost faith and love.'

As she bent to touch her feet, Shahida stepped forward and took her in an embrace. 'Go with the blessings of God, my child. We will look forward to your visits. And don't forget, we are your parents and we will always be here for you.' Shahida then walked up to Virk, her eyes brimming with tears. 'My daughter has seen and suffered what no girl ever should. I humbly beg of you to help erase that part of her life from her memory with your love.' Virk was touched by her words. Their simplicity was beyond his imagination.

'I will, Ammi,' he promised.

Then he looked at the long, curving road ahead, scanning the sea of faces that had assembled to bid them farewell. He continued, 'Ammi, I won't leave any stone unturned, I promise. When we meet you next, you will see a big difference in her. Please have faith.'

Shahida smiled and said, 'I am sure you will. I am a mother after all, and all mothers worry. Go with the blessings of God. May He be your guide, always.'

Minutes later, after the newly married couple was seated comfortably, the vehicles began moving slowly and then picked up speed. They moved from hill to hill where Bibi saw hundreds of villagers, lined up on the side of the road, waving their hands, wishing them a safe journey.

She too waved back till she lost sight of them.

Bibi put her head on Virk's shoulder and said thoughtfully, 'How I wish my parents were alive to see this day. I feel my mother's presence, telling me that she's so happy to see me as a bride. How can I ever thank you?'

Virk was touched by her words. He put his arm around her, pulled her closer and planted a kiss on her forehead. 'Your parents haven't gone anywhere, Amrit. They protected you from harm; they smile and laugh through your lips and eyes. Perhaps, they selected me too for their beautiful daughter. They are with you all the time.'

She was so choked with emotion that she could not reply. She let her husband's priceless words sink into her heart and prayed that what she had heard was indeed true.

It soon dawned on Virk that everything outside the village was new for Bibi. She had never stepped out of Tunda and needed Virk's guidance at every step. He was surprised to learn that Bibi had never travelled by train. There was childlike excitement on her face when Virk told her that they would take one to his home town, Delhi. She sat next to the window, and throughout the journey, she gazed dreamily as the picturesque scenery flashed before her. On many occasions, dust hit her eyes, but she refused to shut the window.

Virk watched her in amusement. He was travelling with his entourage and had booked the entire compartment. His assistants were eagerly waiting at hand to help if they needed anything. This made him more relaxed.

As the night set in, she climbed up to the upper berth, even though there was an empty lower berth, and waved at Virk who laughed at her delight. However, in the middle of the night, she climbed down and sat next to him. He woke up, startled by the movement. 'What happened?' he inquired.

'Nothing. I can't sleep. By the way, you haven't told me who all are there at your home. Will they accept me?'

Virk laughed out loud. The assistant came running, thinking he had been called. 'All okay, Sahib?' he inquired. But seeing them sitting close to each other, he rushed back to his seat in embarrassment.

Virk held her by the arm and pulled her closer. Shy, she hid her face in his nightshirt. 'Stop it, please. What will people say?' she said, trying to wriggle out of his grip.

'They will say that a husband is talking to his beautiful wife because she can't sleep. Now let me tell you about my parents. I am surprised I haven't told you anything about them. They live in Delhi. I haven't told them that we are married. So when we reach home, it will be a big surprise for them. My mother will throw a fit. She'll scold me, shout at me and will be very, very angry. But not with you. She will protect and guard you and hold you close to her heart. In her, you will see your own mother. My father is just like me, or I'm like him. He is happy to see me happy. And that's that. By the way, even he didn't inform his parents when he married my mother. And this was when such things were unheard of.'

This made Bibi even more anxious. 'You haven't told them? What if they don't like me? What if your mother gets angry with me? What if she doesn't let me in? Where will I go?'

Virk realized the intensity of her insecurity. And she had her reasons to be so. Her face was now only a few centimetres away from his. He kissed her on her lips and held her tightly. Tense and embarrassed, she clung to him like a creeper and didn't make any effort to free herself from his grip. 'They know I like you. I have been talking about you ever since I first saw you. It's just that I was always on the move. And for a military officer, duty comes first. You must know, dear Amrit, that come what may, I will always be there with you, always.'

Relieved by his response, Bibi slid her head under his armpit and settled in with him. She was soon fast asleep. A few minutes later, Virk got up and lovingly covered her with a blanket. He looked at her admiringly for a few minutes and then took the lower berth opposite hers. Before lying down, he said, 'I don't know how to pray, O God, but please accept my deepest gratitude and sincere thanks.' Minutes later, he too was fast asleep.

They reached Delhi early the next morning. It was windy and there was a nip in the air. Everyone on the platform, including the coolies, was wearing sweaters but Bibi refused to cover herself with warm clothing. 'I am happy without it,' she told Virk.

Many smartly dressed officers were waiting to receive them at the station. Bibi happily accepted bouquets of flowers as she walked alongside Virk to the waiting car. She was impressed to see her husband being saluted by a battery of military personnel. Soon, they were on their way to her new home.

Bibi was awestruck as the car sped down the mostly empty roads of Delhi. Even though the city was yet to wake up, she was impressed by the colonial architecture, the wide roads and the beautiful buildings of Connaught Place. About half an hour later, their car came to a stop in front of a palatial house. Bibi continued to sit inside the car while Virk stepped out and pressed the doorbell. The night guard, who had dozed off in his cabin, came running out to open the large wrought-iron gate. Virk was about to sit in the car when he saw his mother coming out of the main door. She exclaimed with joy and rushed to meet her son.

Virk too stepped out eagerly. 'How are you, Ma? Didn't go for your morning walk today?' he asked.

Preeti Virk held her only son in a tight embrace and then looked at his face questioningly. 'You've lost weight. Army doesn't feed you or what? And how many times have I told you to inform us before coming? I would have come to receive you. You know I like doing that. Also, the tea at the platform tastes so good!'

Virk smiled and then led her towards the car. 'Allow me to introduce you to someone, Ma. Let me see if you can guess who she is.'

Reaching the car, Preeti looked through the window to find a beautiful and shy bride sitting on the back seat. Her gaze was down but her beautiful face and sharp, attractive features were clearly visible. She pulled open the rear door hurriedly and sat next to Bibi. She cupped her face with her hands and exclaimed with joy, 'You're Bibi Amrit Kaur, right?'

Bibi nodded.

She touched the red bridal bangles on her wrists and then blessed her by placing her right hand on her head. 'Welcome to your home, my child. I have been eagerly waiting for this auspicious day.' Bibi felt overwhelmed by her touch but didn't respond. Her fears left her and she felt relaxed. She bent down and touched her mother-in-law's feet.

Stepping out of the car, Preeti screamed at her son even though he was standing just at arm's length. 'You are so irresponsible! Why didn't you inform us? Who made you an army officer! Now wait here till I come back.' Then, without waiting to hear his response, she ran inside and re-emerged a few minutes later holding a steel plate with some jaggery and a bottle of mustard oil on it. A few pieces of jaggery fell on the ground as she rushed towards her son and daughter-in-law but she didn't care. She handed the plate to the servant and poured mustard oil at the bottom of each side of the gate. Then taking the plate back, she gestured Bibi to enter the house. Bibi was aware of this ritual, having witnessed it on a few occasions at her parents' home. But she felt elated to think that it was happening for her.

She accepted the small piece of jaggery her mother-in-law gave her while saying a quick prayer and then entered the house. She was greeted by her father-in-law, Randit Singh Virk, who was standing in the living room. His eyes were filled with joy. His welcoming smile told Bibi that he too was pleased by his son's choice. He escorted her inside but was not followed by his wife and son.

Preeti had business to settle with her son that couldn't wait. Switching to an angry tone, she looked at him disapprovingly. 'You have a lot of explaining to do,' she began.

'Yes, Ma, let's go inside first; I will explain everything,' replied Virk helplessly.

She softened her tone. 'She's so beautiful and innocent. I am so happy for you.'

'Yes, Ma. I agree. Now let's go in.'

Virk's cold response irked her, 'But why didn't you tell me before?'

'Ma, as I just said, let's go inside. I will explain.'

'Both you and your father are beyond my understanding.'

'Yes, Ma. I am feeling cold. Now let's go inside.'

'Do you know, your father did the same thing. His parents weren't aware of our marriage either.'

'Yes, Ma, it runs in the family.'

'You should have at least sent us a telegram. I don't even have sweets at home. And I am avoiding chocolates.'

'Yes, Ma. I should have. I will explain. And I have brought imported chocolates for you. Let's go inside now. People are watching us.'

'Will you and your father ever change, I wonder.'

'We will, Ma. Now let's go in.'

Satisfied with her rant and having stamped her authority, she went in and sat next to Bibi on the sofa. Both father and son sat at a little distance and watched them as they chatted over tea. 'We have heard so much about you and the challenges you've faced. Please treat me like your mother. Together, we will write a new chapter in your life. Just remember, life comes with a confirmed "return ticket". Therefore, live with a heart filled with joy and not with one filled with pain,' Preeti reassured her beautiful daughter-in-law, who nodded shyly. The new house reminded Bibi of her father's bungalow. There were plenty of similarities in style, upkeep and functioning.

In a matter of days, she settled in the new environment like honey mixes with milk. The city never ceased to amaze her—be it the big American cars, the stylish bungalows or the luxury hotels. Her eyes widened each time she heard the high prices of fruits and vegetables. Her small negotiations with vendors amused her mother-in-law no end. But soon, she got accustomed to her new life and began learning the art of living in a modern society.

She travelled extensively with her husband to numerous army stations and within a few months took control of his life too. The office of the Army Wives Welfare Association became her second home. Talking at length to the wives of the jawans and being involved in their lives gave her immense pleasure. Despite being a senior officer's wife, she displayed no ego and mingled with the women without any qualms. She did not hesitate to break the chain of command to address serious issues and used out-of-the-box ideas to put the soldiers' families at ease. In a few months, her selfless devotion and care made her a household name in Virk's battalion.

Her home too was blessed with harmony, and she received love in abundance from everyone. However, for unknown reasons, Bibi couldn't conceive again, yet no one in Virk's family ever made that an issue. But deep within, her heart yearned to meet her sons. She tried her best but couldn't erase their memory from her mind. This often made her sad and restless. She had no way of finding out if they were okay. As a result, she spent a few hours each morning praying for their welfare. Virk was aware of her pain but was helpless. Despite his best efforts, he could not get any information on them.

* * *

With the passage of time, Bibi became more and more spiritual and spent many hours each morning in meditation. She had just one deep desire—to meet her children.

And just like that forty years passed by, and they were full of happiness and marital bliss.

9

War was brewing on the borders of Punjab. Around the beginning of March in 1965, the Indian Army detected extensive movement of the Pakistani Army's infantry.

* * *

An elegant, suave and strikingly beautiful woman with sharp features and long hair streaked with grey stood in one corner of the officers' mess in Delhi's cantonment area, watching her husband being ceremoniously promoted to a new rank. The two tiny crossed swords on his shoulder flaps were glittering, adding enormous respect and responsibilities. He was now a Corps Commander (GOC) of the Western Command, headquartered in Shimla. And in those days, there were just a handful. The greying beard on his face looked sharp and bright in contrast to his olive-green attire and matching turban.

In his new uniform, Major General Virk looked every inch the handsome, decorated commander. The expression in Bibi's eyes was that of immense happiness, satisfaction and gratitude. She felt proud of the rank insignias on her husband's uniform. He had reached the pinnacle of his career and was the star of the evening. As was customary, colleagues and seniors walked up to him and poured chilled beer over his shirt and medallions. While the practice was to sprinkle a few drops of liquor on the newly promoted officers, it was Virk's popularity, warmth and camaraderie towards his juniors that had melted all the boundaries of formality, allowing everyone to celebrate his promotion. It was their love for the new general officer that had filled the air with cheer. 'Wish you many more!' they shouted aloud as they gulped down mugs of beer in quick succession.

Not wanting to be left out, the women too joined the party with gusto. They raised one toast after another and cheered the tall and lanky sardar. The bandmaster was a seasoned subedar. His eyes didn't miss out the genuineness behind the love and affection on display by both the officers and the ladies. Taking a bit of liberty, he waved the baton twice and abruptly stopped the routine, traditional martial tunes. He swished his baton again and whispered a few words to his band. Reacting swiftly, the musicians began playing pacy Hindi film songs. It was a risk the subedar was taking, for which he could be hauled up by none other than the second most senior officer of the Indian Army. He very well knew that this was an official event being attended by officers in uniform. His act could put him and his superior in deep trouble. But the soldier in him was elated to see an exemplary officer like Virk being promoted to flag rank.

As soon as the music came on, the wife of the general officer commanding-in-chief (GOC-in-C), Mrs Rathod, raised her champagne glass and nodded her head excitedly. Her eyes met with the band members' who bowed gently while the GOC-in-C smiled uncomfortably. Emboldened, the other women too broke into a spontaneous jig. The centre space, adjacent to the spacious, well-stocked wooden bar, turned into a lively dance floor. Mrs Rathod held Virk's hand and led him to the floor. With one hand on her delicate waist, Virk moved elegantly to the rhythm. They danced like nobody was watching, breaking the shackles of hierarchy.

Bibi watched the festivities from her vantage point, wearing a big smile on her face. She held a tall glass of sparkling champagne in her hand, sipping it from time to time. But in reality, she was not a drinker, only pretending to be one. Havildar Ram Singh, her favourite steward, kept replacing her glass with new ones that held less and less alcohol every few minutes so that it looked like she was enjoying her drink. 'It is a big occasion for me, Amrit,' Virk had told her before the party. 'And most women drink beer and wine. Even if you don't drink, just hold a glass so that it seems like you are celebrating with them,' he had pleaded. Realizing what it meant to her husband, she had agreed. Now aware that she would be summoned to the dance floor very soon, she handed the glass to the steward and mentally prepared herself.

As she made her way to the dance floor, the music changed and folk songs began to play. Virk watched her as she tucked in the loose end of her saree in her petticoat and took position with her hands slightly raised. He looked confused but the bandmaster instinctively knew what was coming. As soon as he increased the volume, Bibi started performing the traditional gidda! Her feet stamped the floor in a delicate, measured way, her expressions matching her vigour. Virk was pleasantly shocked to see her perform with such gusto. And soon the stage emptied, letting her perform in complete freedom. Virk had never seen her dance before. It dawned on him that she was emerging from the last of her mental bondages, breaking free and letting go of the enormous pain in her heart. He joined her, matching her steps, and the two entertained the crowd. As the song ended, Bibi pulled Virk in a deep embrace and burst into tears. There was a big smile on her face, but the tears reflected her gory past. The crowd was quick to respond. General Rathod and his wife were the first to clap, followed by thunderous applause from the gathering. Bibi looked into Virk's eyes and gently pulled him towards her. She stood on her toes and planted a kiss on his left flap. 'More strength to you. May you take care of this responsibility to the army's satisfaction.' Her words couldn't be heard by the others but the expressions on her face melted everyone's heart.

Amidst loud cheers and applause, the two stepped down from the dance floor, hand in hand. Virk escorted Bibi to the sofa and then went to the adjoining room. Minutes later, he emerged wearing a fresh uniform and went straight to the bar. He needed to celebrate the liberation day of his better half. Her tears had touched the core of his heart. The bartender poured him a large Russian vodka and while pushing the glass in his direction, he said, 'To your good lady's happiness.' Virk looked at the senior steward, smiled and extended his hand. The bartender shook it and saluted in return. 'I feel so proud and elated to be serving you, Sir. Thank you.' Virk heard him but said nothing in return. Instead, he raised his glass. Being an army officer, he was expected to keep his emotions in check. But he was finding it difficult to control the tears that were threatening to burst out.

When the customary cocktails went on well after lunch hours, Bibi became worried. She was closely watching her husband raising toast after toast. She walked up to him and despite being a few drinks down, he was all ears, 'Take care of your body, dear hubby, it is the only place for your soul to live!' Virk nodded and smiled in return and then, bowing gently while the assembled officers and their wives watched, placed his glass on the table. *Okay, it was time!* He glanced at the logistics officer standing across the bar and gestured to him. It was time to stop. So no more refilling of glasses, and the music was stopped too. The atmosphere changed and the glasses vanished from the hands of the guests. Lieutenant General Rajendra Rathod, the northern army commander, walked in and took the centre stage. Holding the ceremonial baton in his hands, he began addressing the gathering.

'My dear General Virk. It is such a proud moment for me to see you climb up the ladder. We all know what the tricolour means to you. We all know how you wear your heart on your sleeve when it comes to Hindustan. While I would like to compliment you for your sincerity, loyalty, hard work and countless, most productive initiatives, I would also like to share with you that, from now on, a serious responsibility rests on your strong shoulders. Our friends next door are engaging in a serious misadventure, which can have far-reaching consequences. If this is allowed to continue, it could lead to a warlike situation. As the western army commander, it is quite comforting for me to see you at my right hand, in charge of the tactical and offensive operations, especially on the borders of Punjab. Till date, you have not let the grass grow under your feet. It is therefore a privilege for me to stand with you shoulder to shoulder and prepare for any eventuality. It's such a big relief to just have you around. Welcome on board, General Virk!'

The large and beautifully decorated mess, filled to the brim with officers of all ranks, erupted in applause. However, the commander's speech did wipe the sheen from the faces of the women. Possibilities of war and the resultant bloodshed and death of innocent people made them emotional. But having suffered the Partition, they knew well the real meaning of the term 'occupational hazards'. The sit-down lunch began soon after. Maintaining the protocol, Bibi sat next to the army commander's wife, while Virk sat next to the GOC-in-C. The long centre table glittered with silver salvers and fine porcelain. Vases filled with roses and an array of dishes added to the setting. Stewards serving the seven-course meal stood attentively in sparkling white uniforms and matching gloves behind the guests. Their movements were synchronized with the military band playing martial music on the balcony overlooking the dining hall.

Mrs Rathod was in awe of Bibi Amrit Kaur. Besides her breathtaking beauty, Bibi's tales of bravery had been discussed at length amongst the army wives. She was admired and respected for the courage and determination with which she had punished her attackers. 'I feel so happy and privileged to be with you, dear Amrit,' Mrs Rathod said. 'Honestly, I am proud of Virk for proposing to you and feel happy that you are part of our big army family. Please do not hesitate to call me when Virk is travelling.' Bibi mulled over the words and their deeper meaning spoken so casually by the first lady.

She smiled back and said, 'My husband is second only to God for me. To see him around gives me a feeling of fulfilment and safety. It makes me feel complete and secure. I am not sure if it was a reward from the angels for the terrible losses I suffered in my life. But my faith in the Almighty makes me firmly believe that Virk shall emerge triumphant from whatever situation he is put in.' Even though Bibi was careful to respond in a soft tone, her words weren't missed by General Rathod. Breaking the protocol, he pushed his chair back, stood up and held his glass in a toast. His sudden movement took the entire gathering by complete surprise. They all followed suit and held their glasses in the same manner. In the chaos, the stewards realized that many of the glasses their officers were raising were actually empty.

They rushed to replenish them and, in the process, spilled a few drops on the table. The army commander overlooked the commotion as if he had anticipated it. After a brief pause that allowed everybody to settle down and pay attention, he began. 'It is a proud moment for me to share with you what I just overheard Mrs Virk tell my better half. It touches the core of my heart and makes me feel proud, honoured and privileged that we are bestowed with the honour of sitting next to such a refined soul. I would therefore like to raise a special toast in her honour.'

Mrs Rathod raised her glass and looked at Bibi. 'It's plain water, not champagne. You can safely drink to your happiness.'

Bibi smiled and bowed her head realizing that despite all her smart manoeuvres, she had failed to keep her little act a secret. 'Yes, Ma'am,' she said and picked up the crystal glass.

'To you and to your great health and success, Ma'am and Major General Virk!' he concluded as he took the first sip.

'To your health and glory,' repeated the officers in unison and raised their glasses. A round of applause from the women followed, who had remained seated. Partially hidden, a shy Bibi closed her eyes. Her shapely reddish-maroon lips moved ever so softly, 'Thank you, Lord,' she whispered to herself. 'I wish you were here, dear Mother, I miss you.'

* * *

The very next day, General Virk was to leave for Amritsar. Bibi escorted him to the Palam airport and walked right up to the ladder of the military aircraft. Before boarding, Virk turned towards her and looked into her eyes. She stood ramrod straight and looked back confidently. He was surprised to find no signs of worry or fear on her face. Her firm faith in the Almighty had always surprised him. Yet watching her see him off with a brave face astounded him.

Stepping a bit closer, he said, 'Is there something I can get for you? It is quite likely that we might go right up to Tadali. We are quite keen to end these skirmishes once and for all.'

Bibi's face became serious instantly. She stepped closer, and in full view of the officers present, who were watching her closely, she held her husband's hands. Placing her forehead on his chest, she said, 'Please do what you must. That's your duty. But, if possible, please avoid bombarding my parents' home. Their souls might get hurt.'

General Virk was struck by her simple but deep words. The officers too noticed the change on their general's face but couldn't make out what was happening. Recovering quickly and maintaining his composure, Virk said, 'Their house might be in the enemy territory, Amrit, but it is still the civilian area. And unlike the Pakistanis, we in the Indian Army do our best to avoid attacks on civilians.'

Virk boarded the flight without turning and looking back at Bibi. Minutes later, the C-119 Packet aircraft taxied towards the airstrip. Bibi stood at the same spot, her back towards the officers waving at the departing aircraft, her eyes closed, but her lips moving ever so gently. She was communicating with her lord.

A month later, Bibi learnt that Allah Rakha had passed away. She insisted on going there and being with her adopted family. However, most of the sectors closer to the Pakistani borders in Kashmir were under curfew due to continuous shelling. 'It isn't safe, Amrit,' Virk tried to argue with her on the hotline. But Bibi remained adamant. With little choice, Virk made the necessary arrangements, and Bibi arrived in Kashmir much to the pleasant surprise of the villagers.

The women greeted her with love and affection. They garlanded her and gave her a hero's welcome. She was one of them. They surrounded her and engaged in small talk. They were impressed by her dramatically changed and impressive body language. Her clothes were more elegant, her demeanour more mature. Many teenagers touched her repeatedly. She had changed, they felt. It was not the Bibi who had lived among them. She had grown in stature, and they were proud to see her commanding respect from the accompanying military personnel. Yet what touched them the most was her love for Allah Rakha and his family.

Bibi hugged Shahida and burst into tears. Allah Rakha's only son, Abbas, had returned with his family from Nepal a few months ago. Standing in a corner with a sombre expression, he watched Bibi with amazement and disbelief. He had heard many stories about her. But after meeting her, he realized her importance in his family. She attended to the barrage of visitors at the door and performed the rituals like a real daughter would. She did all the chores at home, including serving kehwa to the visitors, without paying any attention to the fact that she was an army general's wife.

A week later, she shifted to Jalandhar, the nearest family station for army personnel engaged at the battle front. The staff had maintained the official quarters really well in Virk's absence and the large, spacious house looked spick and span except for the study. That was the only room in the entire house that was still locked. But Bibi knew where to find the key. She opened it to find books, files, maps and documents scattered untidily on the floor. She began setting the large desk in order. While doing so, a map caught her attention. Intrigued, Bibi placed it under the table lamp and took a closer look. A small black dot was carefully encircled in red ink. It denoted Tadali. She was surprised by what she saw and bent down to read the fine text. In bold ink, Virk had scribbled, 'Amrit Home' on top of the dot. She held the map close to her heart. Memories came rushing back but she didn't lose her composure. 'Thank you so much, dear Virk! I am so grateful . . .' she murmured and sank into the plush chair. The teenager in her was transported to the famous Sardar House in Tadali.

But life did not afford her the luxury of sitting back and thinking of days gone by.

Barely a week later, she had to rush to Delhi. Her in-laws had met with a car accident and were admitted in the army hospital. Despite the doctors' best efforts to save them, they succumbed to their injuries a day later.

Virk flew in for a few hours to perform the last rites but went back the same night. 'A lot is happening on the front. What has happened can't be undone, but I have responsibilities. My country comes first, Amrit. I have to go back,' he said before taking the midnight flight to the base camp.

A week later, Bibi received more sad news from Kashmir. Shahida had passed away in her sleep. Putting on a brave face, Bibi went back to Kashmir and returned two days later after performing the last rites.

Despite these tragedies, Bibi's faith in the Divine didn't waver. She became strong spiritually and spent more and more time in prayer and meditation. In order to stay productively occupied, she shifted to Khem Karan and began teaching at the army school as a volunteer. With every passing day, it became clear to her that Pakistan would attack India. But nothing could force her to go back to Delhi. 'My dear husband is fighting on the front. The least I can do is stay close to him. I have no one else now,' she argued and anchored herself firmly.

* * *

Khem Karan

Shelling on the Punjab border intensified with every passing day. At the army's request, some villagers in surrounding areas began evacuating their houses, but a large number refused to move out. 'It's still peaceful out here, no bombing,' they insisted. 'When it gets out of control, we will shift,' said the panchayat chief in a firm tone. 'We will stand guard too and help you,' said others with patriotic fervour.

The army tried its best but failed to convince them to change their mind. This news reached Bibi's ears. She saw the delicate situation and decided to step in. Secrecy of her going to the villages was maintained but whispers travelled faster than Bibi's jeep, carrying the saga of her bravery. As she stepped into the large compound where the villagers had gathered, the atmosphere became joyous. Her radiant face and genial smile endeared her to all immediately—men stood up and clapped appreciatively while children danced about her. Many touched her out of curiosity or just to feel her skin. The womenfolk garlanded her and sang songs of welcome typical to their region. It seemed like the people of Khem Karan were overjoyed to find the fighter Bibi Amrit Kaur amidst them.

She hugged the women and acknowledged their warmth with smiles. Escorted by her guards, she sat on a big cot that the villagers had cleared for her and folded her hands. The noise and the milling around continued till she settled down. It was clear that even though they had defied the army's request, they were moved by her concern for them and a bit surprised that a serving general's wife had personally taken the trouble to drive down for the sake of their safety. Bibi, in turn, found herself reciprocating the love she had received from the villagers. She had some local snacks that were served and shook hands with young girls who were seated in the front rows.

After a good fifteen minutes of pleasantries, she began to address them. There was grace in her voice and care in her expressions. She talked about how their being in their homes would be an added worry for the army, about how the army could not spread itself thin. She then urged them to move into the army school. 'I admire your decision to stay put in your village,' she said. 'But till the time the situation remains uncertain and dangerous, please stay in the school compound which will be manned by army guards. We will ensure a supply of water, food and other basic amenities.' After completing her appeal, she waited for their response.

The panchayat chief was the first to speak. To the surprise of the escorting subedar and guards, he agreed to her request without any 'ifs and buts' and thanked her for showering the village with care and concern. He also said that if this helped the cause of the army, then so be it. The meeting ended before it could even begin properly. But the villagers were in no mood to let her go back yet. A sumptuous lunch was laid out quickly and she was served like a guest of honour. Looking at the vast variety of dishes, it soon became clear to Bibi that each family had prepared something for the occasion. Shaking her head in disbelief, yet not wanting to hurt their feelings, she ate what she could and carried along packed mess tins that were filled with food and brimming with love.

Two days later, the school began receiving its guests. Young children and their mothers occupied the classrooms that were emptied and made into makeshift bedrooms, while the elders put mats and cots inside the compound. Bibi helped them set up. She converted a large room into a rations store. She also helped them set up a makeshift kitchen. She herself took charge as an administrator. Her physical presence ensured full backup from the rank and file at the army cantonment.

During the day, she and a few other teachers ran regular classes while the men helped the army in numerous chores, including loading trucks with ammunition. But as the war intensified, all activities at the school came to a halt. Movement of troops made it difficult for the army to provide transport to the villagers. Seeing their plight, Bibi herself refused to move out. She vacated the palatial bungalow, shifted into the school compound and occupied the principal's office. A large curtain separated her bedroom from the office that also doubled up as a clinic.

Having been a part of the army, Bibi was well versed in war alarms, sirens and blackout procedures. She painstakingly trained the villagers in emergency drills, digging trenches and firefighting. 'No war can be won if the citizens don't cooperate,' she told them and motivated them to be brave, fearless and firm. This encouraged both the men and women to act as foot soldiers. The ordinary Sainik School was now an additional support base for the troops.

Bibi's presence also had an all-round electrifying effect. Young boys changed their mindset and began dreaming of joining the army. Shy and introverted young girls saw a hero in her whom they wanted to emulate. In a matter of days, an ordinary village transformed itself to stand against the invaders, should the situation so demand. Bibi Amrit Kaur became 'Bibiji' for everyone, and her word was taken as no less than a command. The school was now a well-oiled machine, willing to go to any extent on a single directive from Bibi. She remained active and excessively occupied during the day, but at night she often recalled her journey and the days of Partition when she was left to die by the mob. It was as if life had come full circle. It was she who was in the same position as her father. However, there was a big difference; almost an entire village was ready to sacrifice everything in order to protect her. Although there were no similarities, the school building reminded her of 'Sardar House', her parents' home.

10

It was July 1965. Major General Samarth Singh Virk's jeep came to a screeching halt on the driveway of his house in Jalandhar. Bibi had been escorted to their official residence in the city from Khem Karan earlier. The small, olive-green flag bearing his rank on the front bonnet stopped fluttering. Before the driver could jump out of the vehicle to open the general's door, Virk alighted and rushed into the house to find Bibi standing on the front porch. He looked at her, smiled, but said nothing. She accepted the shining, eighteen-inch-long black ebonite baton from him. Placing it over the wooden stand, she asked, 'What's the matter, you look worried?' Virk tried his best to look normal despite being aware that it wasn't easy to hide much from her razor-sharp eyes. Without responding, he headed to his room. Bibi followed close behind, her ears tuned to pick up even a whisper from her husband's mouth.

Entering the spacious, well-lit but simply designed master bedroom, Virk pulled open the large teak almirah and carefully took out a sealed folder. While untying the cotton tag binding the corrugated box marked 'RESTRICTED' in bold, he looked into her eyes and said, 'I have been asked to oversee the Amritsar sector. We have a serious situation on hand that needs urgent attention. The Pakistanis are armed to the teeth with advanced armoury, machine guns and, above all, the US-built Patton tanks. With our limited resources, it is not going to be easy to stop them from charging into our territory. We are therefore thinking of different strategies, thus the importance of out-of-the-box experiments.'

Amrit was unfazed by his response. 'Will that mean you'll shift base to Amritsar?' she asked.

Virk smiled, admiring both her composure and query.

Her face was bereft of tension and undue excitement. After a brief pause, he said, 'Temporarily, yes. But the operation should not take much time. Those are mostly diversionary tactics. Our main focus is elsewhere. I just want you to know that I may not be able to communicate with you from the front. Please do not worry in these situations. In fact, you should interact more with the families of the jawans and provide whatever help you can,' he concluded.

Bibi heard him but remained calm and nodded gently. She turned and left the room while Virk buried his head in the voluminous bunch of sheets of paper.

She went to the kitchen and came back with a steaming mug in her hand. A smartly uniformed steward followed her, holding a tray of biscuits. Handing over the tea to Virk, she resumed her queries. 'If they are so well equipped in armament, tanks, etc., how are we going to defeat them?'

Virk paused, locked his eyes with hers, smiled and said, 'We are no match for them vis-à-vis equipment, machinery, etc. But remember, it's always the man behind the machine who matters. And the Pakistanis are no match for us. They are only good at shoot-and-scoot tactics. But when it comes to man-to-man combat, we are far superior.'

But Amrit wasn't done yet. She poured some more tea into his mug and pulled her chair closer to his. 'When do you have to go?'

Closing the file gently, Virk put his head on the backrest and took a deep breath. In the meanwhile, Amrit inched even closer. Virk leaned forward and picked up the mug. He sipped the tea and took a bite of the sweet and salty home-made biscuits and then spoke in a normal tone, trying to sound as if it was all routine. 'I only need a few sets of uniform, battle rig and night suits. My staff will take care of all that. You don't need to worry. I don't see this war lasting long. Both countries don't have the financial muscle to stretch it beyond a point. Both nations have to pay a heavy price for Ayub Khan's error.'

Virk paused, enjoying the look of attentiveness on his beautiful wife's face. Before Amrit could shoot off her next query, he began again, 'But Pakistan will suffer the most. By underestimating India, they have already etched their nation's history with a humiliating defeat.' His softly spoken words, filled with confidence, echoed in the room. Amrit felt the aura of his internal strength. Yet she was far from satisfied.

With her knees touching his, her fingers resting on his palms, she continued with her questions, 'All I am asking you, dear Samarth, is when do you have to go?'

Virk looked at her, smiled, placed his left hand on hers and said, 'Now.'

Amrit appeared to be taken aback but recovered immediately.

'Okay, I will make all the arrangements. I will pack some dry snacks, your favourite biscuits and a few tins of condensed milk. When you get bored of hammering the Pakistani Army, these things will bring back memories of home. Please look after yourself, eat well and keep me posted whenever you can. I am sure you will come back victorious. I will pray for your success.'

He was surprised by her calm and composed response but felt compelled to place the tea mug on the table. He stood up. The furniture moved a little and the steel cutlery tinkled. But his eyes stayed glued on Amrit. 'I have known you for a long time, Amrit. You are such a caring and concerned person. You are not only brave but also a very gifted woman who knows the essence of bravery. I am so grateful to have you as my better half, my soulmate.' Taking a step forward, he cupped her face and hugged her.

They stayed in a tight embrace for a few moments. 'You are a noble soul, dear Samarth,' Amrit said, enjoying the firmness of his grip. 'And it is so gratifying to be addressed as your soulmate, something I didn't quite deserve in the first place. You stood by me, helped me fight my part of the war—however internal it was. All I can do is stand by you and pray, which I shall. When you return, you will find me standing here, waiting for you. And together, we will celebrate the new feathers in your cap.'

They walked hand in hand to the waiting jeep. Bibi picked up the service baton from the stand and handed it to her husband. 'May you stay blessed and return with flying colours.' Her words echoed in Virk's ears as the jeep sped out of the bungalow.

* * *

Not too far away, the war room of the makeshift camp of the Command Headquarters near Jalandhar was filling up with senior army officers from various battalions. They were all dressed in battle rig and looked war-ready. Their agenda was to discuss the various options, scenarios and strategies to be deployed for keeping the advancing Pakistani Army in check. Despite the danger of the war looming large, their faces bore no signs of worry. The commander arrived almost at the same time and gestured his colleagues to stay seated. He walked to the front of the table and pulled out a red-tipped narrow wooden stick from its holder. Placing its coloured pointed tip on the dots circled in red ink, he began his monologue. 'Gentlemen, the situation looks grim. There are over 400 Patton tanks in these three positions besides other sophisticated armoury. As you are aware, these are deadly weapons that they have received from the Americans. And we have become the testing ground for both these nations. About 300 of the 400 tanks are attacking this front as we speak and are barging towards Khem Karan. It's almost a free run for them as our armoured corps is not in a position to engage them gainfully. These tanks are spitting fire, bombing civilians, ruthlessly killing everyone in sight and leaving destruction in their wake. We need to stop them by hook or by crook. Suggestions?'

Without waiting for anyone else to comment, Major General Virk stood up. The pen held gently between his fingers rotated slowly. There was complete silence in the large committee room. Placing the pen on the table, he began. 'Sir, we need to immediately open another front.

We should attack Lahore with our full might. This will force the Pakistanis to stop Uncle Sam's armoury from advancing deep into Khem Karan. They are overconfident at this point of time. They wouldn't expect us to breathe down their necks in Lahore and Sialkot. We can keep them engaged and cause heavy damage to their pride, Lahore. This way it would become impossible for them to retrieve their battle tanks. With the surprise element in our favour, we can force them to run for cover. The sooner we attack, the better it would be.'

As soon as Virk finished his short speech, General Rathod quizzed, 'But that would mean crossing the Line of Control, wouldn't it?'

'Yes, Sir, it would,' came Virk's response. General Rathod paused, thought for a while and said, 'Please wait.' Without adding a word more, he excused himself and rushed to his private office. Once inside, he lifted the hotline receiver and said, 'Connect me to the prime minister, please.'

Minutes later, the firm and familiar voice of Prime Minister Lal Bahadur Shastri came through the receiver. 'Yes, General, what's the status?'

Rathod began in a hurry. 'Sir, we will need to attack Lahore in order to stop the advancement of the Pakistani tanks into our territories.' After finishing his brief statement, Rathod waited for the response.

The prime minister said, 'Then what are you waiting for? Please go ahead. Let this be a lesson.'

General Rathod responded with 'Jai Hind' and replaced the receiver. Back in the war room moments later, he stood at the same spot and steered the pointer to the dot circled in red ink on the map. 'Gentlemen, we have received orders to attack Lahore and Sialkot as soon as we are ready. I am aware, General Virk, that all your pultans are eagerly waiting for this very opportunity. Go tell your boys there shall be no mercy. It's our men versus their machinery. Show them what we are made of. I wish you all the best.'

As soon as the area commander placed the pointer back into its holder, the officers stood up and, almost in unison, saluted the general officer. The briefing ended soon after.

A few days after that, the Indian Army tanks were seen crashing into the iron barriers of the Pakistani border, followed by troops who took on whatever little resistance the surprised and shocked Pakistani infantry tried to put up. Within hours, they reached Sialkot and launched a fierce attack. There were heavy casualties on both sides. Despite the home ground advantage, the Pakistani soldiers found it difficult to withstand the Indian Army's relentless onslaught. For days on end, Indian soldiers kept advancing, leaving behind massive devastation. As Virk had expected, the enemy deserted the battlefield and ran for cover, leaving the strategic control of Sialkot in the hands of the Indian Army.

Advancing farther, the 1st Corps' Armoured Division of the Indian Army launched a fierce attack on Phillora. Post a pitched battle resulting in a large number of casualties on both sides, the Indian soldiers set a record of sorts by destroying ninety state-of-the-art Patton tanks. In the process, a large number of Pakistani soldiers suffered severe burn injuries. Hundreds were trapped inside the thick steel-bodied battle tanks and were burnt alive. This shattered the morale of the Pakistani rank and file. Panic-stricken, they left their advanced armoury, weapons, automatic rifles, tanks and whatever else they possessed, and vacated their positions and posts. Hundreds of them were shot in their back while escaping but they kept running away from the battlefield to the safety of their barracks. General Virk arrived on the field and, like a lion in the jungle, stood on top of his armoured vehicle.

What he witnessed would have deterred any weak-hearted soul. Scattered in front of him, till the far horizon, were the dead bodies of the soldiers. The entire field was littered with hundreds of automatic American machine guns. They all looked brand new. Most of them hadn't been used even once. In a pained voice, he whispered to himself, 'Hopefully, you'll be ashamed of your actions, Ayub Khan. Pakistan's history shall remember you for going down on your knees to lose Sialkot.' He stepped down from the tank and walked a few steps till he reached a machine gun lying on the ground. He picked it up to take a closer look. A faint smile appeared on his face as he saw his deputy walking up to him. Virk looked at the young colonel and said, 'Can you believe this? Not a single round has been fired from this beauty. It's still locked.' The officer took the rifle from the general's hand and stepped back. He was smiling, but his eyes were lit with deep admiration for his superior. Virk walked towards a deserted Patton tank and placed his palm on its body. He whispered, 'Didn't I tell you, Amrit, it's the man behind the machine that matters?'

* * *

Sitting far away in the safety of his office in Islamabad, the Pakistani President, Ayub Khan, and his warmongering generals were shell-shocked. Many were twiddling their thumbs nervously. Even in their wildest dreams, the President had not thought that his pride and honour would be so brutally crushed by a handful of ill-equipped and underprepared Indian soldiers. The loss of Phillora and Sialkot were unthinkable and put the entire Pakistani Army in depression. News of mass casualties and the destruction of ninety Patton tanks had made their military a laughing stock among defence experts. Anticipating the worst,

Ayub Khan rushed to the doors of the United Nations and looked for options, including recalling the fleet from Khem Karan. Simultaneously, in conversations with the American top brass, he pleaded for an early ceasefire.

On the Kashmir front, the scenario was quite different and much more favourable to the Pakistanis. On 1 August, its forces launched a full-scale offensive in Chhamb located in Akhnoor to cut off the main highway to the Valley. In the absence of much resistance from the Indian forces, the Pakistani Army took complete control. Comprising primarily Muslims, the Pakistani Army took it for granted that the Kashmiri Muslims would welcome them with open arms and facilitate their takeover. President Ayub Khan, on his part, even hoped that his forces would be able to take complete control of Akhnoor, allowing him to annex the entire Valley.

The Indian Army was taken by complete surprise. It took the forces some time to get their act together. Meanwhile, having taken Kashmiri Muslims' help for granted, the Pakistani Army began celebrating their victory. But that was to be their undoing. Instead of joining hands with them, the Kashmiris played spoilsport and alerted the Indian Army. They gave away vital positions and plans and helped the Indian Army in devising strategies to launch a counter-attack. Being a hilly area, the Pakistanis had no Patton tanks to back them up, nor did they have the much-needed air force backup. On the contrary, the Pakistani Air Force wasn't even informed by its own army of its intentions of occupying the Valley. And by the time its air force was alerted, it was too late.

On 5 August 1965, the Indian Army surrounded the intruders and engaged them in a fierce gun battle. This led to a complete disintegration of the Pakistani Army which scattered and ran helter-skelter, looking for escape routes. To complicate the matters further, the unorganized Pakistani Army soon found that its logistics support base had been cut off. The best option, therefore, was to run, and that's what they did. Dropping their weapons, baggage, etc., they took whatever vehicles they could lay their hands on, including villagers' bicycles, and ran towards the border. A large number of soldiers escaped the artillery barrage and made it to the border. Those who surrendered were taken in as prisoners of war.

Meanwhile, at Khem Karan, the Indian Army deployed a unique but simple strategy to counter the menace of advancing Patton tanks which was given the code name 'Operation Horse Shoe'. Realizing the urgent need of an expert, the GOC-in-C asked Virk to report at Khem Karan for a brief period.

General Virk was apprised of the situation. His force was well in command of the Pakistani borders right up to Lahore. He had time at his disposal. He moved back and began supervising the operation. Nearly 300 fearsome Pakistani Patton tanks were rolling into Khem Karan, bombing and destroying everything in their path. There was virtually no opposition. The Indian Army had not responded till then.

Virk had a plan. 'Let them come,' he told his officers, who were surprised at being mute spectators in hiding even as the Pakistani tanks rolled into the fields of Punjab in large numbers.

Virk directed his soldiers to break open all the small canals spread across the fields of Khem Karan. Going against every protocol and discipline, he drove a tank and bombarded the makeshift dam, in turn risking his own life as gallons of water came gushing down, swallowing everything in its path, including Virk's tank. Virk and his soldiers somehow managed to survive the onslaught of the water pressure and emerge safely but the steel body of his tank didn't. Its turret broke and the vehicle turned turtle. However, this resulted in massive flooding of the paddy fields that made the soil soft and slushy. Overnight, it became un-manoeuvrable. Not knowing what lay in front of them, the Pakistani tanks rolled on to the wet fields and fell into the well-laid trap. The heavy wheels on steel soon sank into the soft soil. Their undercarriages sucked in the slush, resulting in the stoppage of pistons, pumps and motors. As a result, the so-called deadly, menacing and unconquerable battle tanks and the soldiers controlling them became sitting ducks with only their guns operational. Soon the brave Indian soldiers commenced the counter-attack.

Havildar Abdul Hameed of the Indian Army was among the first to show the way. Under the cover of darkness, he crawled on the muddy field right up to the tanks stuck in slush and began shooting at them using his recoilless gun. He blasted three Patton tanks before he was martyred on the Khem Karan battlefield. His valour, together with that of a hundred others, led to panic among the Pakistanis. Instead of fighting back, they deserted the battlefield, abandoning their guns, weaponry and their prized and sophisticated Patton tanks. For the warmonger Ayub Khan, Khem Karan became yet another chapter of shame. So much so that even his best ally, the US, began doubting the potential of its own battle tanks. Havildar Abdul Hameed was awarded the Param Vir Chakra posthumously for leaving behind a trail of destruction and giving nightmares to the Pakistanis for time to come.

The retreating Pakistani soldiers were met by the villagers who were waiting for them at the school. They pounced on them and began hitting them with stones, sticks and other sharp farming tools. Youngsters standing on the school's rooftop shot small stones from their home-made catapults. Bleeding Pakistani jawans ran as fast as they could. On their tail, there were hundreds of sardars, shouting, '*Bole So Nihal, Sat Sri Akaal*!' Bibi Amrit Kaur stood all alone in one corner of the terrace. She was all by herself. Her hands were folded and her lips were moving ever so gently. She was praying, 'O Waheguru, please stop these killings . . . let there be peace, I urge you!'

But General Virk wasn't done yet. Having tasted success at Khem Karan, he called up his colleague engaged at the border of Pakistan Occupied Kashmir (POK) at Haji Peer Pass to get an update on the situation. The brigade commander came on the radio immediately and began briefing the core commander. Having served under General Virk in the past, the brigadier could sense his excitement. Amidst sounds of heavy shelling, he said, 'Sir, the Pakistani Army is finding it hard to match the fierce man-to-man combat launched by our brave men. They have vacated their posts and are running helter-skelter to save their lives. We are now in full control of the Haji Peer Pass, moving towards the borders of Muzaffarabad. Over.'

The brigadier waited briefly and soon heard the general's commanding voice. He was surprised when he realized that the proud core commander had a personal agenda too. 'Mukesh, look at the map carefully. At Muzaffarabad in Pakistan there's a small village called "Tadali".'

The brigadier looked closely, spotted Tadali and shouted back, 'It's there, Sir.'

In a calm voice Virk said, 'We are all aware that the Pakistanis have unethically attacked and murdered civilians. But now that the tables have turned and the tide is in our favour, the entire field is open to us. I want you to ensure that, as far as possible, the civilians and all those surrendering should not be harmed.'

Mukesh's eyes grew big with surprise. A hoard of officers and senior jawans, who were busy making notes, looked at the brigadier with inquisitive eyes. 'Roger, Sir. But anything specific, Sir?' he asked hesitantly.

Virk placed the marker on the desk and said, 'There is this large palatial white haveli, known as "Sardar House" that falls under the civilian area. It belongs to my wife.'

Brigadier Mukesh Kumar replied, 'Roger, Sir, it shall not be touched. Regards to Ma'am, over and out.'

The very next day, General Virk sent a message to Bibi Amrit Kaur. 'We are not too far from your home. Even as the Pakistanis have raised white flags and are running like hares to Tashkent and the UN to save themselves, I want you to know that we have tried our best to not kill civilians. Your house is safe too.' Bibi read the message repeatedly before placing the paper in the drawer. She sank into a chair and unintentionally went down memory lane. Her eyes were shut but images from that day flitted through her mind. She could hear the cries of her mother pleading

127

with her father, 'Don't leave us alive, Balwant . . .' Her screams were louder than the chants of the rioters who were banging on their entrance gate. They were shouting out aloud, 'Kill the Kafirs . . .'

With some effort, she went to the bathroom and splashed her face with cold water. After wiping it dry, she stood in front of Guru Nanak's picture with folded hands. Tears flowed freely down her pink cheeks. 'I pardon them all, O Nanak. I want to avenge no one. Please end this war. Let every mother see her son alive. May good sense prevail everywhere!'

In September itself, a defeated Ayub Khan signed on the dotted line, timidly admitting defeat, which in turn brought an end to the bloody war. General Virk came home to a hero's welcome and became a celebrity among his peers and seniors. However, he also began facing health issues. Due to his close proximity to the loud sounds of bombs going off, he became partially deaf. His lungs were badly affected due to excessive inhalation of gunpowder. And in addition to these were the injuries he had received due to the dam water hitting his tank with full force at Khem Karan.

In 1970, Virk took premature retirement from the army to focus on his health. Over the next two decades, Amrit and Virk shifted to the Valley and would walk from Allah Rakha's home, where they had decided to stay, to the gurdwara every day. In 1993, Virk suffered a heart attack and died a week later, culminating four decades of his journey with an angel who had come into his life as a refugee.

By then, Bibi had become an evolved soul. She accepted Virk's passing away as part of destiny and tried to move on in life. She was sixty-four years old by then but in good health, capable of looking after herself. Like her father, she too started a free education programme for underprivileged girls. She used all her money and savings in providing the village children with whatever help and care they needed. She was alone but never lonely as she immersed herself in the life of that tiny hill village. Soon, everybody came to know her as 'Badi Bibi'. Most villagers, especially the children, couldn't even recall her full name. 'Bibi' became a title, synonymous with motherly kindness.

11

Even in her quiet, religious life, Bibi never forgot her children whom she'd been forced to leave behind. And now that life had rendered her alone again, she was filled with the memories of her boys. She longed to see them. When hostilities between India and Pakistan ceased and peace prevailed, she applied for a Pakistani visa to visit the Sikh holy shrines. This would be her reason to visit. She believed that as long as she had God by her side, she would be okay.

Staying at the far end of the Valley and therefore not having easy access to consulates or even basic connectivity, she used the services of an agent who had befriended her at the gurdwara. The broker offered to arrange a visit to Pakistan and convinced her of a trouble-free, month-long trip. In return, he demanded a whopping fee of twenty thousand rupees and promised to deliver the passport and visa to her home within a month. A gullible Bibi believed him and agreed to make the monetary arrangements.

Over the next two months, she sold her remaining jewellery and took up numerous assignments, including designing bridal dresses for Kashmiri girls. 'It's of no use to me,' she told Arif who protested against her decision to sell the last of her heirlooms. As the word spread, almost the entire neighbourhood found unique, subtle ways to contribute. Bibi's small apartment soon turned into a makeshift designer boutique for the village women. However, the old wooden staircase to her house couldn't bear the weight of so many people and soon gave way. The women asked their respective husbands to help and, without wasting any time, all the carpenters of the neighbourhood were summoned. The repair work was timed with Bibi's daily visit to the gurdwara. In just two hours, the old structure was replaced with a new one. It was also given a fresh coat of green paint. Bibi was deeply moved by the kind gesture of the villagers and thanked them profusely.

On his part, the broker kept a sharp eye and frequented the gurdwara in order to keep himself updated on Bibi's collection drive. He flaunted his connections with important people living in cities and strategically leaked his pictures with VIPs and politicians. As soon as Bibi was able to put together the required sum, he arrived with his wife and collected the money from her. The women, who were present as witnesses, even clapped and congratulated Bibi. The agent pocketed the money and left with a promise to return within a month.

And that was the last time she saw him.

Bibi was left high and dry but she took the setback in her stride and moved on. Even though the entire village cursed the broker and his family, there was no regret in Bibi's eyes. 'If that's what the lord wants, then so be it,' she told her well-wishers and tried to calm them. She stayed firm in her mind, and she didn't look pained or dismayed even once. Nothing could shake her belief in God. Her daily visits to the local gurdwara, come hail or storm, continued. Her story came to be known in the entire region. Parents used her devotion to and belief in the Almighty as an example to share with their children. Bibi maintained her monologue with God that she should not die before meeting her sons. For the next eight years, not a single day went by when she did not present herself at the doorstep of the gurdwara. But she received no sign. Yet her faith stood firm. Deep within, she was aware that God was listening, that it would happen.

Seasons changed but her resolve only strengthened. One winter, in the month of March, the Valley received so much snow that all the roads got blocked and people had to trudge through six-foot-deep snow. Heavy landslides around the area made it almost impossible for Bibi to even step out of her home. But her determination and willpower remained unflinching. She nailed together wooden planks to make a flat, three-foot-wide board. Satisfied with her work, she sat on the board and pushed herself forward using a small flat stick and manoeuvred around the landslide. She almost fell into the steep valley a few times but miraculously escaped from the jaws of death. She somehow managed to reach the gurdwara. By then, she was completely exhausted, breathless and drained. Still she mustered all her strength and shovelled the soft snow that had collected at the entrance door. After she had cleared the area, her eyes fell on the metallic lock hanging from the latch. The wooden stick fell from her hand and she fell on the ground, hitting her head against the door. She managed to get up and sit on the steps. Suddenly, it dawned on her that it was too cold for the old Granthi to come to the gurdwara.

She sat under the concrete canopy and faced the heavy snowfall. Her frail body shivered in the cold but she was determined. Pulling her bare hands out of her shawl again, she knocked on the door even though it was locked from the outside. Her hands were cold, weak and powerless, but the knocks emitted a loud sound. She spoke out aloud to drown the sound of the wind. 'O Waheguru, I am here because I have no one except you. I have nowhere to go except your home. And I have no one to speak to other than you. You know it. Then why are you testing me like this? Why do you want me to fail? What have I done to face your wrath? I am not going to give up, or get up from here until you respond.' Saying this, Bibi sat down resolutely and covered her face with her thick black shawl to protect it from the bitter cold. Soon her entire body was covered in soft white snowflakes.

At the same time, not too far away, the Granthi was uncomfortably tossing on his bed. 'Bibi must have reached the gurdwara,' he murmured to himself. 'I must go and open the door, else she'll freeze to death . . .' Mustering all his courage, the old man stood up. He took one final look at the fireplace and the warmth it was emitting. But his mind was made up. He turned towards the door and pushed it open. The sudden gust of wind brought in tiny snowflakes that settled on his silver beard. Not letting the cold deter him, he stepped out straight into the blizzard. Holding a walking stick in one hand, he began his short but demanding journey to the gurdwara. His feet felt heavy and every step he took seemed like an onerous task. 'Bibi will be waiting . . .' his lips kept uttering as if chanting a mantra. These words gave him strength and he pushed his aged body forward, one foot at a time. He fell many times but refused to give up.

The gurdwara was only about fifty feet away from his house, yet the walk was no less than a marathon for his aged, frail body. After several minutes, he reached the entrance to find Bibi sitting on the steps. With frozen, shivering hands, he pulled out the key and flung open the door. He helped Bibi stand up and dusted off the snow that had settled on her head. 'Please go inside, Bibi. Go meet your Waheguru. Tell him to have mercy on you and me too. I am sure he won't find another devotee like you in the entire universe.'

Once inside, he hurriedly lit a fire in the fireplace and settled down, knowing well that Bibi would spend a lot of time talking to her God. The dry wood caught fire quickly, in turn spreading warmth to all corners of the small room. Rubbing his palms, he turned to look at her and found her in deep meditation. He walked up to her, draped a thick woollen blanket around her shoulders and then got busy preparing kehwa to keep himself warm. She didn't move or get disturbed. Her eyes remained closed. Her heart was beating ever so gently. She looked in complete peace with her Waheguru.

Amidst the complete silence and dim lights, the priest could feel a strange glow around Bibi. He had never witnessed such a phenomenon before. *Is this a figment of my imagination?* he wondered and kept staring at Bibi. She was surely communicating with God but her lips weren't moving. Yet he could feel the presence of an energy surrounding her. He closed his eyes to listen to the sound of silence and be a part of this mysticism. He thanked God for giving him the strength and courage to travel the distance. The experience was invaluable, serene and surreal, yet magnetic, pious and unexplainable in words. 'I wish to merge with this divine serenity forever, O God,' he prayed.

There was no question of Bibi returning to her home that night. She prayed and meditated as if there was no tomorrow. The priest stayed awake too, to witness with his own eyes every single moment of Bibi's spiritual journey. *Thank you, God, for rewarding me so graciously,* he repeated many times in his mind. Sometime around midnight, Bibi lay down, folding herself into a small bundle, and went to sleep. The priest stood up, and, without making any noise, went closer. His eyes scanned the right side of her face, hands and feet. They were all milky-white and flawless. Even though her eyes were shut, there was an amazing aura around her face.

Lifting the blanket softly, he covered her body and then went back to the fireplace to add more wood. He then returned to where Bibi was resting and sat down next to her. His lips didn't move, his eyes remained shut and his hands folded, but his heart was praying for Bibi. *O Lord, this child of yours has travelled a long journey and performed every task you asked her to. She has only one desire—to meet her children before she dies. Please, I humbly pray, grant her this wish. I seek nothing else.* By then, the small prayer hall had become warm and cosy. An hour later, the priest too fell asleep.

* * *

The screeching sound of tyres against asphalt woke him up. He looked around to find Bibi sitting in the same meditative posture as she had the night before. He observed that the entire stock of firewood had been consumed to keep the room warm through the night. He picked up the remaining sticks, broken branches and wood scraps and shoved them into the fire. He stirred the flickering embers with an iron rod, reviving the fire. A honk from outside made him look up. He walked to the window to see a caravan of military trucks moving slowly. The one in front was clearing the snow to provide a clear passage to the following vehicles.

The snowfall had stopped completely and the valley was bathed in warm sunshine. 'Oh, I slept for too long!' he exclaimed aloud in surprise, breaking Bibi's concentration. She opened her eyes, bowed at the holy book in front and walked towards the priest.

'I am thankful to you, Sir, for coming to my rescue yesterday. Without that, I would not have survived the cold.'

'It's all by God's grace, Bibi. I did nothing,' he responded and went towards the door. His sharp ears had picked up the gentle knocking. 'Who would come in such conditions?' he murmured as he pulled the wooden doors open.

'Bhaiji, is Dadi Ma inside?' Arif asked with a worried face. The innocent look in his eyes touched the priest's heart.

'Yes, son, she's here. Come in,' he said softly.

The boy hurriedly took off his shoes and ran to where Bibi was squatting and hugged her from behind. 'Dadi Ma, someone has come to meet you. He has brought your passport. It is stamped with the visa for Pakistan. Baba wants you to come home and sign some papers.'

Bibi heard him patiently but, surprisingly, didn't show much excitement. The priest jumped up with joy and came running. 'Your prayers have been answered, Bibi! Go, meet your children. Honestly, I can't believe this is happening. It's as if God himself decided to descend on earth to answer your prayers. Go, Bibi, don't delay!'

Bibi remained quiet. She walked up to the holy book and knelt down. Her forehead touched the soft white cloth covering the carpet. Her lips were moving, but there was no sound. She was conversing with her God. Both were talking, it appeared, yet there was complete silence. She stood up a minute later, held the young boy's hand and began walking towards the door. The priest watched them leave and then closed his eyes and prayed. 'Please, O Lord, help Bibi meet her family. I pray to you.'

The priest continued to stand in the same spot for several minutes. His hands were folded and his head was slightly tilted. He was looking at the spot where Bibi had placed her forehead. There were two wet spots right where she had placed her eyes. With a prayer on his lips, he walked towards them and sat down. 'She has only you, O Lord. She doesn't know anyone else. She remembers you day and night and has unflinching faith in you. Please listen to her, look after her and travel with her. Thank you. I am so grateful.'

It was the priest's last prayer. Soon after, he fell to his side. His eyes were shut, his soul had departed, but his face exuded calmness as if all his prayers had been answered.

Later that evening, the entire village gathered and cremated him with honour. All through the ceremony, Bibi stood in silence as a mute spectator. But she shut her eyes as soon as the pyre was lit and began murmuring, 'May you be with God, dear Babaji. May your soul be free . . . May you rest in peace . . .' She bowed gently, turned around and started walking in the direction of her house.

The sun was setting on the far horizon behind the mountains, filling the valley with bright colours. 'Take me to you, O Lord, but not before I hold my children in a tight embrace. The mother in me still wishes to feed her infant children who were snatched away by destiny. My soul still hurts. I know you are listening. Please help, I pray to you, O Father. Thank you.'

12

Amrit had fulfilled all her duties, as a wife, as a daughter to her birth parents, as a daughter to the parents who had adopted her, her in-laws, and her God. The only thing left for her now was to meet her children. This was what was keeping her alive. And now she was closer to her goal.

As she packed a small handbag of her belongings, she showed no sign of excitement. Her face was as calm as it had always been. She knew this was a 'do-or-die' situation; her last opportunity, but she wasn't agitated or perturbed because she knew her lord was by her side.

She climbed down the stairs and knocked on Allah Rakha's door. His younger grandchild, Altaf, opened the door and looked at her for a second and then ran inside to inform their father, screaming, 'Baba . . . Baba . . . Dadi Ma has come.'

Soon Abbas, Allah Rakha's son, was at the door, welcoming her inside. 'Please come, please step in, Bibi. So happy to see everything has finally fallen in place.'

Bibi looked at the house as if she were seeing it for the first time. She knew every inch, every corner, but today it all seemed different. She looked at the kitchen and could almost feel Shahida's presence, walking towards her with a teapot, offering kehwa to the young Virk. 'Please look after my daughter,' she could hear her say. 'Help her in erasing the past from her mind.'

Her lips broke into a smile. Her gaze shifted to the sofa and she remembered how Virk had sat gingerly on its edge, talking to Allah Rakha, making promises while seeking Bibi's hand. Her cheeks turned crimson as she remembered the happy moments. *Virk was a rare gem,* her heart whispered to her ears, and her eyes closed in agreement. Abbas was looking at her, letting her relive old memories. He loved and respected her and felt her presence would bless the house.

Suddenly, screams from the children broke Bibi's chain of thought. She sat down on the cot and saw Arif, the elder grandson, emerging from the adjoining room holding a mug filled with kehwa. Accepting it, she gestured to the younger one. The young boy, Altaf, came running and sat down next to her. Placing her hand over his head, Bibi said, 'Here, this is for you. When you grow up, live with your family and look after them.' Saying this, she pulled out a small, handmade, maroon velvet cloth pouch and placed it in his tiny hand.

'What's this, Dadi Ma?'

'It's a small gift for you,' she replied with a big smile.

Altaf opened the pouch with great excitement and pulled out a key. Holding it in his hand, he looked at his father questioningly. Abbas intervened. 'Bibi, please don't do this. You'll come back. You have to come back. We want you to come back. This is your home and it always will be. Arif will travel with you to Amritsar and wait till you return. Go and come back safely. We pray, have always been doing so, that you meet your children and hold them in your arms. May Allah grant what you have been looking for all your life . . .' He then looked at his elder son and said in a polite but firm tone. 'Go with her, Arif. Look after her. Remember, this trip is more important than any religious pilgrimage for her. And you cannot perform a better Hajj than ensuring that she returns home safely.'

'Yes, Baba!' he said as both men stood up and walked to the door to see Bibi off.

Before boarding the bus, Bibi went inside the gurdwara and prayed. Arif sat next to her obediently and together they listened to the *Shabad* (holy songs) being sung by the *raagis* (singers): '*Koi bole Ram-Ram, koi Khudai, koi*

Sevai Gosaiyaan, koi Allahe . . . [some recite Ram-Ram, some remember Allah, while others call upon their Gods, whereas He's just the One omnipresent . . .]' After the song ended, Bibi stood up, went to the raagis and handed over two bundles of hundred-rupee notes. 'By the grace and command of Waheguru, I am leaving this in your custody. Please use it for running the school in the gurdwara. May God be with you.' She bowed in front of the holy book and spoke to the Almighty in her mind. *'Tera shukar hai, Rabba. Teri raza wich mainu apne aakhri safar di ijaazat deyo* [I am grateful to you, O Lord. Under your divine grace, please permit me to perform my last journey].' She bowed again and with a cheerful face, stepped out of the gurdwara.

They took a bus to Delhi and from there a train to Amritsar. Frail in health but mentally strong, energetic and upbeat, Bibi's eyes scanned the faraway horizon as if searching for the familiar faces of her sons. At Amritsar, Arif escorted her to the immigration office and helped her with the clearance. He watched her till she disappeared from sight and waved at her even when he knew she wasn't looking at him. He felt depressed and happy at the same time, as if a part of his own heart had chipped off and drifted away. 'May Allah bless you and help you in uniting with your children, Bibi . . .' he prayed with his head touching the ground.

A hawker standing nearby was looking at him with much interest. 'Sir, you look like a Muslim, and she's a Sikh. I saw that you prayed for her. What is the secret behind this strong relationship?' he finally asked.

Arif smiled. 'Bibi taught me the true meaning of the adage: "*Ekas ke hum baarik* [We are the children of one God]." Our religions are made by us and we often get steered towards hatred due to lack of education. We get brainwashed by fundamentalists. It's spirituality that connects us to God and not religion. Bibi treated me like her own child, without ever bothering about caste and creed. She's travelling to Pakistan today in search of her two sons who are Muslim, and I am going to wait here till she returns. There are no compulsions and yet we're there for each other. Simply put, pure love is not bound by any religious preference.'

The hawker nodded but before he could grasp the deep-rooted essence of the traveller's statement, Arif shot him a query. 'Sir, can you please suggest any low-cost accommodation for a week?'

The hawker thought for a moment and then lifted his hand but then quickly lowered it as if he had changed his mind. 'Sir, would you please consider staying with me? It's a small but neatly maintained one-room house. I assure you, you will be comfortable. I live alone, and I have no bad habits. I have Lord Krishna's pictures in the room. Hopefully those won't bother you?'

Arif smiled and said, 'Back home, Bibi too has them, and those of Guru Nanak as well. She's no less a saint herself. She taught us the true meaning of an omnipresent God. Nothing else matters to us now. I am obliged by your kindness, and I will feel privileged to be surrounded by the pictures of Lord Krishna.'

13

From Attari, the bus travelled fifty kilometres out of Lahore to Hassan Abdal, popularly known as Gurdwara Punja Sahib by the followers of Guru Nanak. A historic place of worship, it is visited by millions of people from many faiths including Muslims, Hindus, Multanis, Sindhis and Sikhs. It is said that Guru Nanak stopped at Hassan Abdal during his travels for a few days to preach the essence of '*Ik Onkar* [One God]'. One of his disciples, Bhai Mardana, a Muslim saint, became thirsty and went to Wali Qandhari, a self-proclaimed owner of the reservoirs and natural streams in the area. Sitting on top of the hill, Wali saw Nanak addressing a large congregation. He felt a pang of jealousy seeing the influence of an ordinary-looking man dressed in simple clothes over the masses.

When Mardana approached Wali and requested for water, the latter threatened him with dire consequences and shooed him away. A dejected Mardana made two more futile attempts. Helpless and thirsty, he finally went to his guru and pleaded for help. 'I am dying of thirst, Baba, please help.' Having given ample opportunities to Wali Qandhari to release the water voluntarily, Guru Nanak walked a few paces and reached a spot where lots of small and big rocks were scattered around. It was a dry, sandy area. With the sun beating down fiercely, it was difficult to even stand barefoot in the open. But the guru didn't seem to care. He squatted on the rocks and began praying.

The innocent and humble villagers were curious. They were mesmerized by his aura and began pinning their hopes on the guru. They were impressed by his simple yet meaningful sermons. His voice had an inexplicable magnetism. It seemed as if his eyes could cut through the walls of the past and pierce the future. In him they saw their messiah who had the power to resolve their biggest problem—the water scarcity created by Wali Qandhari who controlled the reservoir on the mountaintop.

Nanak continued to sit on the big rock and sing praises to his God.

Wali was dumbfounded by Nanak's strange actions. Mardana was also aware of his guru's spiritual powers. He still looked confused as he had never witnessed his guru do something so strange. Scratching his beard, he kept his eyes glued on Nanak's every movement. After a few minutes,

Nanak stopped singing. He simply bent down, effortlessly picked up a large stone and tossed it aside. It rolled over scores of pebbles and settled amongst other rocks. The inquisitive villagers followed the rolling stone till it came to rest. But when nothing happened, they looked at each other, wondering what had occurred.

And just as they were beginning to give up, a big fountain of fresh water erupted from beneath the earth's surface, exactly from where Nanak had displaced the stone. The stream sprang high up in the air and fell on the parched, sandy earth with a gush. The sudden burst took everyone by surprise. In utter disbelief, the crowd retracted at first but then, recovering almost instantly, ran towards the fountain. Their flat, dry and dusty palms felt the cold water. Their tongues caught the droplets mid-air to realize that indeed it was the priceless shower of life. Many lay down on the wet surface while others cupped their hands and drank the sweet nectar to their heart's content. Having quenched their thirst, they began collecting the precious liquid in their containers.

The water continued to flow freely in a steady stream and soon created a large pool at the foot of the mountain. The villagers realized that their deep desire to have their own reservoir had been fulfilled. Ecstatic and filled with joy, the innocent, humble and poor farmers began dancing. Their bare feet hit the wet soil and tiny droplets splashed on their sunburnt faces. Water had been scarce, but now, their livestock wouldn't die of thirst, their children would be able to quench their thirst at will and they would have sufficient water to grow their crops. They even momentarily forgot the saint who had made this happen.

Guru Nanak quietly moved away and sat on a bigger rock at some distance. He had a prayer to say. He needed to thank the lord. A shell-shocked Mardana sat on the edge of the pool, his hands folded under his chin, his feet immersed in water. His heart was filled with gratitude. He felt blessed to be accompanying a true saint on his travels.

The incident had, however, caused an upheaval at Wali Qandhari's house. His reservoir began emptying rapidly, making his followers panic. Scared of the consequences and fearing the wrath of their master, they ran around like headless chickens. Before Wali could act, the large, deep pool filled to the brim with fresh, cold water emptied out. He was stunned. He carefully scanned the reservoir from one corner to the other. All the outlets were tightly shut. There were no signs of leakages either. And yet the water had disappeared. 'How did this happen?' he screamed in rage.

His ego was crushed, and he stood shamefaced in front of his own followers. Seething with anger, he mustered all the magical powers he possessed and rolled a massive rock down the mountain slope. The boulder went crashing down at breakneck speed. Like a homing missile, it rushed towards Nanak who was sitting not too far from the newly created pond below the mountain. He was unperturbed by the commotion around him. His eyes were closed. He was meditating and singing the name of God, blissfully unaware of the rock coming towards him.

The villagers saw the boulder coming towards them and ran to safety. But Mardana rushed towards his guru, shouting out loud to warn Nanak. Unperturbed, Guru Nanak waited till the black granite rock reached arm's length, and when it did, he simply extended his right hand and placed his palm on the surface of the rock. The large boulder stopped in its tracks and came to a grinding halt. Nanak removed his palm, stood up and walked away. But the impression of his hand got embedded on it as if it were not granite but a piece of soft wax.

Shocked and dismayed by what he had witnessed, Wali Qandhari threw aside his staff. He had realized the power of Guru Nanak. He rushed down from the hill and fell at Nanak's feet. 'Forgive me, O holy man. I seek forgiveness. Please pardon me. I stand defeated,' he pleaded. Nanak, the merciful, blessed him too and directed him to use his gifted powers for the welfare of the people instead of abusing them for his personal gain. For many centuries thereafter, the Moguls, the Britishers, the fundamentalists, the radicals and scores of others tried their best but failed to destroy the hand imprint on the black stone. The site soon acquired a holy status. With each passing decade, millions began pouring in for prayers. As a result, the gurdwara boundaries had to be expanded to accommodate the pilgrims. They all believed, and continue to do so, that whoever visits Punja Sahib and prays, his or her wishes come true.

Bibi was the last to enter the gurdwara. With a walking stick in her hand, she walked slowly and observed everything around her. As she reached the outer gate, she stopped and looked back. Amidst the large crowd, busy in its daily chores, she found herself alone. The pilgrims travelling with her had already entered the building. They were all eager to see and feel Nanak's hand imprint on the black granite. The market outside, on the other hand, was completely unconcerned with what was happening inside the gurdwara. The shopkeepers were more interested in meeting their daily targets. Hundreds of small shops were engaged in conducting brisk business and outdoing the competition.

As Bibi scanned the bazaar, she pondered, *How will I find my children in this melee? I don't even know if they settled down here in the first place. Where should I start?* A few minutes later, she turned towards the gurdwara, took two steps into the boundary line and bent down to touch the soil with her fingers. Placing the same hand on her head as a mark of respect, she sought the blessings of her lord and softly said, 'O Nanak, thank you for bringing me here. Over fifty years have gone by. Help me locate them. Without you, I won't be able to find them. Please, Waheguru, I beg you. I know you'll not send me back empty-handed.'

Inside the gurdwara, the devotees had already set up their musical instruments. The Shabad-kirtan (songs of prayers) had begun. And almost all the pilgrims were participating with much gusto. Bibi sat with her back against the wall, admiring the interiors designed by Afghani Sikhs who were forced to migrate to Pakistan due to the uprising of the Taliban in Afghanistan. These Sikhs had camped inside the gurdwara for a few years and waited for the uprising in Kabul to settle down. Despite having limited resources, they had restored the interiors of the gurdwara and given it an extraordinary sheen. They had spent hundreds of hours embedding thousands of small, round mirrors in the walls, ceiling and the inside of the dome. The pieces of glass twinkled like stars, throwing reflections of the pilgrims. Bibi could see a serene and colourful facade that changed with every new entrant. But it took her no more than a few minutes to get back to her prayers. She moved away from the wall and sat in her regular posture. Her back was now erect and her eyes were closed to all the glitter around. Her mind, heart and soul were together again. And her lips were uttering her only request to God.

Searching for her sons was like looking for a needle in a haystack, and she knew that. Her children themselves were now on the verge of becoming senior citizens. Yet her face bore no expression of worry. She was in complete command of all her faculties and at peace with herself, as if she knew more than a soothsayer could foretell. After an hour or so, she exited the premises and went to the community kitchen to help cook food for the pilgrims. After the meal had been prepared, she washed the utensils, cleaned the floors and then went to her allotted quarters inside the gurdwara. It was a small room constructed along the long wall of the temple. The room had no window. One side was occupied by a wooden cot with a cotton mattress and the other by a small almirah. The bed sheet was old but it looked clean and ironed. Bibi kept her small cotton bag on the bed, took out her towel and went for a bath. Half an hour later, she went to where the black granite stone was placed. It was half submerged in water but the handprint of Guru Nanak was clearly visible. She stepped down the stairs. The pond was filled with colourful fish. They were used to humans and freely swam around the pilgrims' feet.

Upon reaching the stone, she placed her right hand on top of the imprint. Her fingers fit in and merged with those of Nanak's. 'Thank you, O Nanak, for bringing me here!' she said. 'If it was not for you, I wouldn't have been able to survive this long. I know you'll not send me back empty-handed. It's just that the mother in me is too eager and impatient to hold her sons close to her chest. I am sure you'll understand.' Bibi paused for a moment. There was no one behind her. The water was ice-cold, which is why the other pilgrims had taken a quick customary dip in the pond, touched the stone and made an exit. But Bibi was in no mood to get up. Giving vent to her pent-up emotions, she continued to talk to her lord. 'I also wish to seek forgiveness for hurting my attackers. Please pardon my acts. I have long forgiven them for what they did. Bless me, O Nanak, to stay alive till I meet my family, I pray. Thank you, Waheguru. I am so grateful.' Satisfied with her monologue, she drank some water from the pond and stepped out. Her clothes were soaking wet, but she showed no signs of feeling cold. Barefoot, she walked back to her quarters filled with new energy.

Back in her room, she quickly changed and then went to the kitchen for lunch. Unknown to her, an old man had been quietly observing her all along. He looked deeply impressed by her devotion. He sat down next to her. They looked at each other, exchanged pleasantries and ate their meal in silence. Most of the pilgrims had finished by then and had left the langar hall. The food was simple. It comprised rice, dal (lentils) and mixed vegetables, but it was so tasty that Bibi took two helpings and instead of a spoon used her fingers to enjoy it.

The old man observed that she was crying and tears were falling in her plate. In order to hide them, she had covered her head as much as she could with her dupatta. The old man waited for her to finish, and when she did, he stood up and picked up her empty plate from the floor. Bibi looked up in disbelief, but he calmed her down, 'Allow me the privilege, Bibi,' he said softly. There was a reassuring familiarity in his voice. She let him have his way but her eyes followed him all the time.

The old man carried the utensils to the sink, washed them and placed them neatly on the rack. He then went into the kitchen and came back with two cups of tea. Bibi accepted the beverage and settled on the chair. After a brief introduction, she narrated her story and sought his guidance. The old man looked at Bibi in disbelief. Placing his mug on the floor, he said, 'Faith can indeed move mountains. But what you're seeking, Bibi, seems impossible. However, your journey thus far, riding on your deep devotion and belief, tells me that I am yet to learn many things. I shall pray that you are united with your sons soon. May God bless you!'

Bibi didn't respond with words but bowed with folded hands. Then adjusting her dupatta and placing it neatly over her head, she stood up and was about to leave when she saw the aged Sikh picking up her cup from the floor. She tried to stop him from cleaning it, but knew by then that it was a futile attempt. She thanked him and bid him goodbye before heading towards the exit to begin her search. Stepping out of the premises, she looked yet again at the huge crowd. She began by talking to the shopkeepers. She had an old photograph of her first husband. She showed it around and told whoever would lend an ear that her husband, Sakhiullah, had shifted to Hassan Abdal from Muzaffarabad in 1950 with their two sons.

The shopkeepers and onlookers were amazed by Bibi's story. They were equally surprised to hear her speaking in the local dialect. Some found her request to be filmi. Some responded with a query, 'Are you originally from Pakistan, Bibi? How did you get separated?' A few even sympathized, but soon dispersed and melted into the crowd.

'Perhaps she's deranged,' said an onlooker sarcastically.

'Yes, I am from Pakistan, was separated due to unforeseen circumstances,' she responded so softly that her own ears could barely hear it. She kept moving, not disheartened by the lukewarm responses she received. It was a precious business hour for the shopkeepers and they felt irritated by her queries. Some rudely shooed her away, and called her senile. Others displayed helplessness and disinterest. Not one to give up, Bibi kept walking, stopping and asking anyone who seemed remotely interested in her story. She covered the entire market in three hours but nothing came out of it. Dejected, she sat down on the parapet. Her feet were aching, her heart was weeping and her spirit was on the verge of dying.

Then she looked around and saw a vendor serving hot tea in small earthen cups. She looked at him. The old man, wearing a long salt-and-pepper beard, smiled and said, 'You look tired. Let me serve you some tea and biscuits. You'll feel better.'

'No,' replied Bibi quickly. 'I am not carrying any money, Bhaijaan. Some other time. Thank you.'

But the vendor wasn't going to give up. He poured hot tea into a cup and arranged biscuits on a plate. He then carried the tray to Bibi. 'You must have come to pay obeisance at the holy Punja Sahibji. And to serve pilgrims is a very pious task. Please accept this as a small token of service. I shall be grateful.'

She smiled and accepted the tea. The old man sat next to her holding the tray in his hand. Overwhelmed by the humility of an ordinary and simple-looking roadside vendor, Bibi began chatting with him, explaining the reason for her visit. The vendor, Aleem Khan, tried to jog his memory but failed to match any face with that on the paper in Bibi's hand. 'Oh, I am sorry, Begum Sahiba, but it would not be possible to trace your husband and two grown-up sons, who by now would themselves be in their sixties just by their names or this old picture. I understand what you are going through, but, honestly speaking, you're wasting your time. Only Allah can help you. Please pray.'

Bibi had seen that coming and said, 'I know, Baba, but this is my only chance. I am old and don't know for how long I will live. I don't want to give up. I am sure someone will help me.'

The tea vendor empathized and said, 'Perhaps one of these shopkeepers can help?'

Bibi shook her head and lowered her gaze. But the experienced old man understood what she didn't put in words and said, 'It reminds me of an anonymous couplet, "*Lafzon me hee pesh kijiye apnepan ki davedariyaan. Ye shar-e-numaish hai, yahan ehsaas ke johri nahin rehte* [Describe only in words your claims of belongings. It's a bazaar, this city. Jewellers who value sentiments, don't live here]."'

Bibi looked impressed and nodded her head in appreciation. 'Well said, Baba. You have just rekindled my hope. Thank you.'

After finishing her tea, she was about to get up to leave when Aleem Khan spoke again, 'Recently, Muzaffarabad suffered a severe earthquake. A fundraising camp is being organized by a Sikh boy. His name is Jassi Lailpuria. I have also offered money for this noble cause. Since I did not have the cash handy, I'd asked him to give me some time, so he will come today. You should meet him. I am sure he will be able to shed some light on your situation.'

The tea vendor's words filled Bibi's heart with hope. Exclaiming with joy, she said, 'Thank you so much, Baba. I am sure there will be some good news for me.' Her feet were suddenly filled with new-found energy. At least there was some lead. She headed back to the gurdwara and straight to her room. She changed out of her soiled clothes and went to the laundry room to wash them. She stirred the soapy water with her hand, creating small bubbles. This brought a smile to her face. She gently picked up the biggest of them on her forefinger and admiringly said, 'Please, Baba Nanak, don't let the bubble of my hope burst!'

14

The next day, Bibi woke up early. The night sky was waiting for the first light of dawn to shatter its darkness. There was no one inside the gurdwara when she entered. She switched on the lights and was greeted by her own reflection in the tiny glass pieces that adorned the walls. She smiled and began cleaning and sprucing up the entire place. An hour later, she sat in a corner and closed her eyes. By the time she finished her prayers, the hall was filled to the brim with pilgrims. After her prayers, Bibi went into the community kitchen to help make breakfast for the worshippers.

Over the next two hours, she worked tirelessly, attending to people, serving food, washing utensils and sweeping the langar hall. Sitting in a corner, the old man, who had befriended her the day before, watched her with admiration. He closed his eyes and began praying. 'Please grant and fulfil her wish, O Baba Nanak. She has no one except you.'

As he got up to leave, he came face to face with Bibi. She smiled, folded her hands and said, 'You're rich when you're in the prayer of others. I am so fortunate, Sir. Thank you so much. I am grateful.' Then, without waiting for his response, she walked away to attend to other chores. The old man was stunned. He stood motionless for a few minutes.

How did she know I was praying for her? I am sure she was not in earshot. Thank you, Nanak, for sending a pure soul, he murmured to himself.

Bibi went back to the market outside the gurdwara to begin her search. Hers was now a known face. The shopkeepers were amused to see her again. They smirked when they heard whom she was looking for—a Pakistani Sikh boy. They ignored her yet again. A few passers-by stopped to listen to her story. But it was mere entertainment for them, and none of them had any useful information to offer. Bibi constantly scanned the listeners' faces for a positive reaction but failed to find any. Unfazed, she walked right up to the end of the bazaar till she reached the tea stall. It was closed and there was no one around. She asked a few people about Aleem Khan, but they knew nothing about his whereabouts. She turned around and started walking back to the bazaar. By the time she arrived, the hustle and bustle had picked up tempo. Being a Friday, there were more people in the market.

The shops were doing brisk business. Bibi's query was therefore becoming an impediment for many shopkeepers. Unperturbed, Bibi pressed on, step by step, from one shop to the next, ignoring the irritated looks she received in return. But unlike yesterday, she wasn't tired. Her eyes were filled with new hope, as if she was subconsciously aware of how the day would finally unfold. Suddenly, the loudspeaker on top of one of the minars of a mosque nearby began blaring out aloud, 'Allahu Akbar . . .' It was the call of the muezzin. The bazaar reacted with alacrity. Many shoppers and shopkeepers began preparing for namaz. Scores of shutters started to come down in quick succession and people began heading for the masjid.

As the street became less crowded, Bibi spotted a young boy who was sitting on a motorbike. He was surrounded by a dozen men wearing white skullcaps. He was different from the rest. He stood out in his black turban. She rushed towards him. Reaching closer, she saw that the young man was wearing a round-necked T-shirt over which hung a pendant. It read 'Muzaffarabad'. She bowed gently and without waiting for him to respond, hurriedly said, 'Son, my name is Bibi Amrit Kaur. Are you from Muzaffarabad? Is your name Jassi Lailpuria?'

Hearing his name from a rank stranger, and that too a foreign-looking lady, a shocked Jassi almost jumped up and stood with folded hands. With some hesitation, he said, 'Yes, I am. How do you know my name?'

Bibi ignored his query and unleashed a volley of questions. 'Can you please help me find my husband and children? Here is my husband's picture. And my sons' names are Qasim Zaid and Karim Zaid. They settled somewhere in Hassan Abdal after leaving Muzaffarabad. Please, can you help me locate them?' Bibi sounded excited as if she had found the missing key to her treasure chest. Her frail forefinger was still pointing at the locket around the young man's neck. Then, without giving him an opportunity to answer, she continued, 'Son, I have come from India. I lived in Muzaffarabad with my foster father, Moulvi Syed. My husband's name is Sakhiullah. In the year 1950, I was separated from my husband and two sons. We all happily lived in Muzaffarabad, but I was deported to India due to the Nehru–Liaquat Khan agreement. I have been looking for them since then. Can you please help me?'

Jassi looked flabbergasted. Shaking his head, he said, 'Bibi, by now they must be in their sixties. How can you search for them and, more importantly, how will you recognize them? It's impossible!'

Bibi folded her hands and looked at the young boy with tearful eyes. 'I am already nearing eighty. I don't know how much more time I have. Can you please help me in some manner to locate my children? I shall be deeply indebted to you.' Saying this, she bent down to touch the young man's feet.

Embarrassed, Jassi hurriedly stepped back. Then holding her by her shoulders, he said, 'Please don't do this, Bibi. I shall do the best I can. Please give me a few days. But how will I reach you in case I find them. Also, can you please give some more details of your family members?'

Bibi felt relieved and began, 'This is the address where we last lived in Muzaffarabad.' With a weak smile on her face, she pulled out a paper from her cotton bag. 'Here, son, I am in Pakistan for the next three days and after that will be in Amritsar on this number. I will remain there till you call. I will eagerly look forward to hearing from you. May God bless you.'

Jassi looked at the paper and carefully placed it in his wallet. His eyes were moist. He sat on his motorbike and drove away, leaving behind a hopeful Amrit. She looked up at the sky and said, 'Thank you, Lord. I am sure with your help he will be successful in his search.' She slung her bag across her right shoulder and adjusted the chiffon dupatta over her head. She then turned to thank the shopkeepers and bystanders who had gathered around her and were watching the unfolding of God's miracles with amazement. Almost all of them had folded their hands.

Their expressions had changed too. Their heads were now bowed and the sarcasm had given way to admiration. But Bibi was detached from all this and did not pay them much attention. She bowed with humility and went back into the gurdwara to pray for the young man's success.

Jassi drove straight to his brother Manjit and narrated the entire incident. 'Six decades is a long time,' replied Manjit. 'How are we going to trace them? We don't even know where to start. I understand her desperation, but you should have thought a little before agreeing to such a request. Do you even understand the meaning of making such a promise?'

Jassi didn't respond, knowing well that his elder brother would come up with a solution in the end. Later that evening, after finishing his work, Manjit made a few phone calls, asking friends and acquaintances about Bibi's husband and sons. Replacing the receiver on the cradle after over two dozen phone calls, he looked at Jassi and said, 'Someone has advised that we should meet Baba Syed Zaid. He knows almost everyone from the Zaid community and also maintains a record of their addresses. You should meet him. This seems to be the only way forward.'

Jassi nodded in agreement. 'Yes, brother,' he said and headed towards his room. Bibi's tearful face continued to haunt him. He went towards the photo frame on the wall and prayed quietly. 'Please help me, Guru Nanak. Let me earn good karma by helping this mother meet her lost family after decades of separation.' He removed his locket and placed it on the study table. The word 'Muzaffarabad' etched on the copper plate shone under the light. He ran his fingers over it and sat down on the chair. A few minutes later, he looked up the telephone directory and dialled a number. 'Assalam walekum, can I talk to Baba Zaid, please?'

Jassi reached Baba Zaid's home early the next morning. He was a simple man with an ordinary lifestyle. Jassi looked around the modest living room as he waited for Baba Zaid to join him. It contained basic furniture to seat six guests. But everything was maintained neatly and spotlessly. A few pairs of slippers were placed at the entrance which implied that all visitors had to remove their shoes before entering the living room. Baba Zaid walked into the room a few minutes after Jassi's arrival and after exchanging pleasantries came straight to the point. After listening to him patiently, Baba Zaid stood up from the cot and went inside the bedroom. A little later, he emerged with a register in his hand and sat at the same spot. Flipping through the pages, his frail and aged forefinger stopped at a serial number against which the name Sakhiullah Syed was written.

He opened the corresponding page but the ink had faded to such an extent that nothing could be made out.

Jassi copied whatever telephone numbers he could on a piece of paper, thanked the old man profusely and left in a hurry. After reaching home, he shared his findings with Manjit. The two brothers sat down across the table and began dialling every number on the list. The exercise brought disappointment on their faces at regular intervals. Not letting this dishearten them, the brothers kept talking to strangers and left messages where they couldn't communicate with the concerned person. On the fourth day, a gentleman by the name of Farhat Zaid called back.

'Hello,' he said and, without exchanging greetings, added, 'Qasim Zaid now lives in Swat. He is quite a well-known personality. Both the brothers have retired. Their children are now in command. So you'll find them at home most of the time. They would be very happy to meet you.' Manjit didn't get an opportunity to thank Farhat as he disconnected the line after delivering the message. He handed over the piece of paper on which he had scribbled the information to Jassi and told him how to take it forward.

The next day, Jassi drove for over four hours to Swat district. It was a picturesque, touristy hill station. He was welcomed by an unpolluted, cool breeze which was a pleasant change from the polluted city air he was used to. After making a few inquiries at roadside shops, he made his way to the address he had been given by Farhat. On reaching the house, he disembarked from his bike, stretched his back and looked around. It was a large, spacious and well-maintained house that was built like a haveli. A few cows were tied in the vacant plot on the left due to which the whole area smelt of cow dung. Not too far away, a caretaker was sprawled on a cot. A long wooden stick lay beside him.

At first, the caretaker glanced lazily in Jassi's direction. Then seeing a well-built sardar walking towards the haveli, he stood up in a hurry and grabbed the bamboo sick. He rushed towards Jassi and inquired in a curt voice. 'What do you want?'

Jassi smiled in return and said, 'Is this Karim Zaid's house?'

'Yes, it is. Whom do you want to meet?' replied the caretaker, sizing Jassi up.

But Jassi didn't respond or wait any further. Extending his right arm, he reached out for the doorbell and rang it twice.

The watchman seemed confused by Jassi's confidence. Not sure how to react, he waited for the door to open.

An old but well-built man with a white beard and well-oiled hair stepped out and looked at Jassi. He was wearing an off-white Pathani suit and looked like the family patriarch. Seeing a Sikh boy standing at his front gate, he glanced at the caretaker who shrugged. 'Sahib, I kept asking him for his identity, but he did not listen. Instead he went ahead and rang the bell.'

The man dismissed the caretaker with a gentle movement of his hand and turned towards Jassi. He had an authoritarian manner. He looked every inch a zamindar or head of the panchayat. From his appearance, he didn't look very amused, his body language indicating that he wished to send away the unwanted visitor at the earliest. He walked towards Jassi and stood in front of him like a bull preparing to charge.

'Assalam Walekum,' Jassi greeted and waited for his response.

'Walekum Assalam?' Qasim's reply was a question. 'My name is Qasim Zaid. What brings you here?' he asked curtly.

There was a smile on Jassi's face which irritated Qasim even more and made him impatient. He repeated his question. 'Don't just stand here and smile. I have other things to do. What do you want?'

Jassi extended his hand and said, 'Sir, I am Jassi. I have driven all the way from Hassan Abdal to share important news with you.'

The word Hassan Abdal sent shivers down Qasim's spine. His expression changed. He stepped forward and held Jassi by his shoulders. Shaking him slightly, he asked, 'Are you Bibi Amrit Kaur's son?'

Jassi had expected such a reaction, but still felt shaken up. The firmness of Qasim's grip made him a little nervous. He managed to say, 'No, Sir, I am not, but you could consider me one.' He'd barely finished his sentence when the old man let go of his arm, turned and ran inside, screaming out aloud.

'Karim, Karim. Come out. Bibi Ma has been located. Come quickly! Where are you?'

His leather sandals flapped against the marble floor. He stopped inches away from the big cot lying in the centre and shouted again, 'Karim, where are you? Come quickly, hurry up, hurry up.'

Jassi could see the commotion that broke out from his vantage point. Many women came out from different directions in the house and gathered around Qasim. They looked perplexed and visibly shaken. Some were openly crying. Some were so baffled that they dropped whatever they were holding, the clang adding to the din. Finally, a man who must have been Karim Zaid came out.

'Where, where, Bhaijaan?' His scream was louder than that of his elder brother, his excitement more intense than all the others assembled in the veranda. Qasim Zaid suddenly realized that he had left the messenger at the main entrance. He ran back to where he had left him, held his hand and ushered him in. 'Please, you're most welcome, son. You are like an angel to us, who has brought us such great news. I have waited for this day my entire life. We're very grateful to you.'

Jassi climbed the steps and walked towards the assembled family looking at him expectantly. Escorted by the brothers, he was made to sit on the large, colourfully decorated traditional charpoy. Tens of small brass bells were hanging from it, giving it a festive look. The brothers sat on the floor on either side and began pressing his knees and feet, much to Jassi's embarrassment. Taken aback by the strange behaviour of the two elderly men, the women appeared shocked at first, but when they got to know the gravity of the news that the stranger had brought them, they too fell in line.

'Tell me, son, where is my Bibi Ma? How is she? Does she remember us? Can you take us to her? We will be forever grateful to you, will give you whatever you wish in return for this one favour!' Karim Zaid said excitedly. Qasim Zaid was so overwhelmed that he burst into tears.

A few older women rushed towards Qasim and placed their hands over his shoulders. 'Please control yourself. You will meet your Ammi very soon.' One of them then looked at Jassi and said, 'We are indeed grateful to you for this long-awaited news. My husband and I have always prayed to Allah for her well-being. How is she and where can we meet her?'

Jassi hadn't quite expected such an emotional outburst. Holding himself together, he managed to say, 'Bibi is well and in good health. She has been desperately searching for you all and her husband, Sakhiullah Sahib. I met her at Hassan Abdal and promised to do my best in locating you. For the past four days, my brother and I have been dialling every possible number of your community. Finally, last evening, we got your address from Farhat Zaid. My brother asked me to leave at the earliest. And here I am. Can I also meet Sakhiullah Sahib, please?'

The sudden change in their expressions told Jassi what had happened but he still waited for their response. 'Baba passed away just three months ago. But he was quite certain and repeatedly told us that come what may, Bibi will come to meet us. Please take us to our Ammi, we request you,' Qasim pleaded with folded hands. Tears were rolling down his face in a steady stream like a small child wailing for his mother. But he couldn't care less. Sitting opposite, Karim Zaid wasn't looking any better, but was finding it difficult to express himself. This sudden development was too much for him to handle. Some stranger had just arrived at their home and told them what he had been waiting to hear all his life. His hands kept pressing the feet of the young sardar who was feeling overwhelmed and awkward by the respect that was being bestowed on him.

Seeing the patriarchs of the family crying, a few women too started sobbing. Jassi found it difficult to hold back his emotions. A lump was forming at the back of this throat. 'I am so fortunate to be her messenger. Let me take you to her. She'll be so happy to meet you!'

The brothers stood up with alacrity and ran inside to change into fresh clothes. Meanwhile, three younger women came out of the kitchen with trays laden with dry fruits, biscuits and snacks. 'You have travelled such a long distance, Bhaijaan. Please have some lassi while Abbu and Chachu come back,' requested one of them.

'Please eat something. We will feel so honoured,' said the other.

An overwhelmed Jassi was finding it difficult to process such pure, selfless love. He enjoyed the hospitality of the Zaid family till the brothers emerged from their rooms. They waited impatiently while Jassi finished. He burped loudly before standing up much to the amusement of the women. He then bid farewell to the family and left for Hassan Abdal with the Zaids' car in tow.

To the two sons, the distance seemed twice as long. They cried and talked about destiny and their mother and exchanged stories from the past till they reached the gurdwara. As soon as they arrived, they rushed out and ran inside, only to learn that the group their mother had come with had returned to Amritsar the previous evening.

Dejected and heartbroken, they hugged each other and sobbed uncontrollably. People gathered to watch the spectacle in utter disbelief.

Making way through the gathered crowd, the Granthi stepped forward and separated them. 'I spent some time with Bibi while she was here. I don't know how, but she was sure you'll come searching for her. She hasn't gone too far. She is just an hour away from the border in India. Here are her contact details. Please talk to her, tell her that her sons are equally eager and desperate to meet her. She will feel relieved,' saying this, the aged Sikh handed them a piece of paper. 'For me, it's a miracle that she managed to find her children after so many years of separation. What has surprised me the most is that she was sure of meeting you both! She is a very rare, pious soul. Go talk to her. She's waiting for her sons.'

Karim Zaid grabbed the paper and read it carefully. A shopkeeper standing nearby intervened and said, 'I have a phone in my shop. It has international calling. Why don't you call her right away? Your mother will feel so happy.' Qasim nodded, thanked the stranger and followed him into the shop with Karim and Jassi in tow.

Qasim dialled the number a few times but the call didn't go through. He looked helplessly at the shopkeeper who took the receiver from his hand. 'Sometimes, it's easier to dial Honolulu than connect with India,' he said and began dialling the number but got the same result.

Karim stepped in and said, 'Let me try, please.' At the third attempt, the call went through. 'Hello!' he screamed, loud enough to shatter the windowpanes of the shop.

'Hello,' came the response from the other side. 'I am Arif this side. Are you Jassi?'

Karim's face lit up. 'No, no, I am Bibi Ma's son, Karim. May I please talk to my mother?' Qasim snatched the receiver from his hand and said, 'I am Qasim, Bibi Ma's elder son. We both want to talk to her, please. Where is Bibi Ma?'

Listening to their loud voices, a lot of spectators gathered outside the shop, including those who had ignored her requests and said she was senile.

Many put both their hands up in air and said, 'Allah has his own ways. What a sight this is. No less a blessing!'

A feeble but clear voice soon came through the receiver. 'Hh . . . hh . . . hello. I am Bibi Amrit Kaur. Are you my son?'

'Ammi,' Qasim managed to say before bursting into tears.

Karim grabbed the receiver and said, 'I am Karim, Ammi, I am Karim, your younger son. I was only nine months old when you left, but there hasn't been a day when I haven't remembered you. I miss you, Ammi, want to meet you. Please come back.'

He'd barely finished the sentence when Qasim took back the receiver, but couldn't speak.

He could hear his mother sobbing. Arif came on the line and said, 'We will be in Amritsar. Bibi has already given her passport and contact details to the Sikh baba at the gurdwara. Please get her another visa so that she can come back to Pakistan to meet you as soon as possible.' Standing next to Karim, Qasim too heard Arif speak but before he could respond, the line got disconnected.

He was dejected that he could not hear his mother's voice and tried dialling her number a few times but couldn't get through. Handing over the phone to the shopkeeper, he pulled out a bunch of hundred-rupee notes and gave it to him. 'Here, Sir, please accept this as a small token.' The onlookers looked surprised to see so much money being paid for just one phone call.

But their eyes widened with shock on hearing the shopkeeper's response. 'How can I charge for helping a son talk to his mother for the first time in sixty years! I feel blessed. Thank you. May you have a happy reunion very soon.'

During the homebound journey, Qasim was unnaturally quiet. Seeing his elder brother in this state made Karim restless and he decided to break the ice. 'Bhaijaan, let's approach Mushtaq David. He's the minority minister. He will help us.'

Karim's words did the trick. Qasim looked at his younger brother and smiled. 'Yes, Chotte, let's meet everyone who can help us. Let's go!' And the car suddenly picked up speed.

But things were not going to be that straightforward.

For the next three months they kept knocking at the minority minister's door. 'Nothing works here without cash,' they were repeatedly told. But the brothers camped outside till the minister's staff relented and gave them an appointment. Mushtaq David finally called them in and said, 'She's Sikh, this lady you both want to meet so desperately. And you both are, mashallah, good Muslims. You still want to invite her to Pakistan and take her home?'

Qasim Zaid heard him patiently. Then with folded hands he said, 'I have learnt that Allah is but the only truth. He's the doer and has no shape or size. He was never born and he will never die. He's omnipresent. And we are all his creation. To us, our mother represents that God. Now why he made our mother Sikh and us Muslim, we don't know; and it really doesn't matter. We have suffered for the past six decades. We have been praying to Allahtala to bless us with at least one meeting. Our father passed away recently. But till his last breath, he hoped to meet his beloved wife, told us to never give up. And now, by Allah's blessings, we have found her. Only you can help us. So we beg you to help us get her a visa for Pakistan. She is old, frail and not in good health. Please, help us, please.'

Mushtaq was amazed to witness such love. He called out to the peon, who came running in and said, 'Please take these gentlemen to Faheem Akhtar. Ask him to speak to me.'

'Jee, Huzoor!' the peon answered, and respectfully escorted them towards the door.

As soon as they left, Mushtaq picked up the intercom and impatiently waited for a response from the other end. 'Jee, Janab,' came the response.

'You must answer the phone quickly,' Mushtaq rebuked his personal assistant and then said, 'I have sent you two people. Deal with them. See what they can pay and talk to me before you finalize the deal. Understood?'

'Jee, Janab.' His words echoed in Mushtaq's ears as he placed the receiver and murmured to himself, 'Not a bad start to the day,' and rang the bell again. 'Send the next person in,' he ordered and began looking at his files.

15

Sitting on a cushioned green leather chair, Faheem looked at his two prospective clients and tried to analyse their financial worth. He meticulously took down all the passport details of Bibi Amrit Kaur and began his standard monologue where he tried to show off by dropping names. 'You see, Qasim Bhai, normally the minister does not interfere in the matters related to the ministry of external affairs. He is obviously touched by your story and wants to help. But, as you know, the external ministry wouldn't even look at such matters without some consideration. In my opinion, for five lakh rupees, they can be made to agree to grant a month-long visa to your mother . . .' He stopped and looked at the two brothers for their reaction.

Karim was aware of the standard practice of granting such favours. But he had no clue it would be demanded in such a crude manner. He placed a plastic bag on the table while Qasim engaged the PA in negotiation. 'Sir, with great difficulty, we have managed two and a half lakh rupees. This is all we have. Please, somehow manage within this?'

Faheem posed like a professor in a classroom wearing a thinking cap. A brief moment later he said, 'Okay, please wait outside. I will call you in. Let me make a call. I will have to convince some people that yours is a genuine case. Please leave the bag here.' Then, as soon as the brothers left the room, he took possession of the bag, counted the money and placed it hurriedly in the drawer. Satisfied with his drill, he picked up the intercom and dialled the buzzer.

'Yes?' came the crisp, commanding voice of Mushtaq David through the receiver.

'Janab, party is with me. But they can't afford more than two lakh. I have done a background check. They have borrowed what they could. They can't afford more than this. Besides, it's a good cause. It will give you mileage. I think we should give them some concession and be considerate.'

'Hmm . . .' There was a brief pause. 'Okay, do it. After all, we are here to help the public.'

The clicking sound indicated that the line had been disconnected. Placing the receiver back into the cradle, Faheem rang the bell. A peon appeared.

'Call those two back. Also bring along two cups of tea and some biscuits. Hurry up.'

The peon promptly replied, 'Jee, Huzoor!' and vanished.

He went up to the brothers in the waiting room and said, 'I have good news for you. Your work has been done. Please come with me.' Filled with joy, the brothers stood up but found the peon blocking the way. 'Sahib, *kuchh chai-paani* [tip]?' Karim hurriedly fished out a fifty-rupee note and gave it to him but he did not budge. 'Sir, I have been with Faheem Bhai for many years. I pleaded your case and impressed on him the need to help your cause. Just fifty rupees?' Karim looked at Qasim and gave another hundred-rupee note. The peon pocketed the money but wore a long, dissatisfied look on his face. He led them to the PA's room and closed the door. A minute later, he entered the room again and placed teacups in front of them. The tea was cold and the biscuits never arrived. It was a clear indication that the tip given was below expectation.

'Bhaijaan . . .' Faheem began. 'I have spoken to my contacts in external affairs and the home ministry. Your work will be done. Consider this a miracle. But I warn you. No one should know about this money transaction or your mother will never be able to enter Pakistan. Is that clear?'

Karim Zaid broke the family protocol and spoke first. 'Sir, we won't utter a word. And thank you for accommodating our request. We are truly grateful.'

'Good,' replied Faheem and stood up. 'You can come back next week and collect the letter. Based on that, she can arrive in Pakistan on compassionate grounds. She will be issued visa on arrival. Ask her to carry the letter that the ministry will issue soon.'

'Thank you so much, Sir!' Karim Zaid said. 'We are so grateful!'

They were about to leave when the PA spoke again. 'By the way, what business are you in?'

Qasim replied, 'Sir, we trade in sugar.'

Faheem reacted instantly. 'Oh great. I have a marriage function coming up in the family. Please send two to three bags of sugar to my house. Here's the address.'

Qasim nodded, accepted the business card and exited the room. As they walked along the long corridor, they saw a hoard of visitors waiting to meet the PA. Each one carried a small bag that they held close to their chests, the contents of which were now known to the brothers.

As soon as they left, Faheem pulled out the plastic bag from the drawer and hurriedly removed 50,000 rupees from it. He placed the remaining two lakh rupees in a briefcase, locked the drawer and headed towards the minister's room.

'May I come in, Sir?' Mushtaq looked up, saw the briefcase and gestured him to carry on with what seemed to be a standard procedure. Faheem opened the minister's leather briefcase and placed the bundles neatly in it and said, 'Janab, could you please call the home ministry? I will then follow up and ensure their mother is received here without any bottlenecks.'

'Okay,' said Mushtaq and picked up the receiver. 'Connect me to the secretary of the home department.'

A few minutes later, sitting in his office, Faheem was giving the passport details of Bibi Amrit Kaur to the home department officials and justifying the urgency.

A week later, Qasim Zaid was asked to come and collect the travel documents. Holding the approval letter in his hands, he kissed it many times and thanked Faheem profusely. Back in his car, he looked at the packet and said in a sad tone, 'Oh my Allah, I wonder what they will do with so much loot? Aren't they scared of you? Aren't they worried that they will have to be answerable to you for all this?'

Two weeks later, the brothers waited outside the arrival lounge at the Islamabad airport, eagerly looking at every aircraft that landed or took off. They had heavily tipped the airport staff to get special access to the VIP area. The airport staff was bending over backwards to fulfil their wishes. The word had spread amongst the workers that a Sikh mother was meeting her two Muslim sons for the first time after Partition. As a result, a hoard of spectators had gathered at the arrival lounge. Each vied for a vantage point, eager to see a rare reunion between an Indian mother and her two Pakistani sons.

A large number of off-duty customs officers in sparkling white uniforms also joined in. In their entire career, they had never come across a case where an estranged family was reuniting after almost six decades. Everyone seemed eager to witness the reunion. A few newspaper journalists were also present. Their presence egged on the on-duty airport officials to put up their best act. Bibi's arrival turned into a win-win situation for numerous agencies, including the airport staff.

Soon, an eighteen-year-old boy came running to Qasim. He was a loader on duty, assigned to offload the passengers' luggage on to the conveyor belt. He sneaked through the rubber flaps, ran on to the conveyor belt and stopped right in front of the brothers. Addressing Qasim Zaid, he said, 'Sahibji, Sahibji, I just saw your mother getting down from the aircraft. She has boarded the bus. She will be here soon.'

Qasim Zaid held the boy's face in his hands. 'May Allah bless you. I have waited for six decades to hear this!' Then stepping away slightly, he removed the thick gold ring from his forefinger and handed it to the boy. 'May you never be separated from your mother!' All the workers and officials standing close by began clapping on hearing Qasim Zaid's heart-warming words. Many women broke down and could be seen wiping their tears. A dozen cameras began flashing. The show had begun.

Javed Ishtiaq, the head of immigration, was standing amidst the crowd in civil clothes and observing the drama as it unfolded. 'Ya Allah!' he said aloud. 'May no one be separated from their loved ones like this!' Moving quickly, he went past the immigration checkpoint and the long queues of passengers. He spotted the old lady and went straight up to her. 'You're Bibi Amrit Kaur?' Bibi looked at him closely and realized that he was too young to be her son.

'Yes, I am.'

'Please come with me. Your sons are eagerly waiting for you,' he said excitedly and then added, 'Welcome home, Bibi.'

Bibi found it difficult to hold herself together. Thanking him and Waheguru at the same time, she followed the officer and tried to keep pace with the help of her walking stick. The immigration officer saw his boss accompanying a female passenger. He stamped her passport without looking at it and let them through. The waiting area was still a good fifty feet away. Javed raised his hands and gestured to the brothers and the two women accompanying them. They came running and stood in front of the officer. The officer stepped aside, and Bibi came face to face with her sons.

'Bibi, meet your children, Qasim Zaid and Karim Zaid,' saying this he stepped back. The brothers were dumbstruck for a moment. And then, they stepped forward and hugged their mother. She threw away her walking stick and wrapped her arms around her sons. They held each other tightly and cried their eyes out. The onlookers started clapping, giving her a resounding welcome.

Bibi had nothing in the way of luggage except a handmade cloth bag. Escorted by her sons, their wives, grandsons and daughters-in-law, she went past the green channel. A long row of musicians was standing on either side of the red carpet laid by the brothers. They were playing the popular Hindi song, *Baharo phool barsao mera mehboob aaya hai* [Shower flowers, O springtime, my beloved has arrived]'. The loader dashed through the crowd and tapped Qasim gently on the shoulder. 'Sahib, here's your Ammi's walking stick.'

Qasim took the cane and threw it away. 'From now on, we are her walking stick. She won't need this any more.'

Amidst the bustle, they managed to reach their cars and were about to get in when the chief immigration officer came rushing up. 'I believe that Bibi was deported from Muzaffarabad. I have spoken to the authorities. She is most welcome to visit her ancestral home and live there. And if she desires, she can stay for up to three months instead of a month. Necessary formalities will be completed soon.'

Qasim Zaid was speechless. He shook hands with Javed and thanked him. As their cars exited the airport, the crowd that had assembled outside waved at them.

After a few days of rest, Qasim asked Bibi if she wanted to visit the Sardar House, the place of her birth. To his surprise, Bibi refused. 'I won't be able to live those moments again,' she said. Instead, she shifted to Muzaffarabad along with her entire family and moved into the same house where she had lived after she married Sakhiullah. En route, she stopped at the police chowki, stood in silence outside the main entrance and sought forgiveness. As she turned towards her car, the constable on duty saluted her. He had been told who she was, and he seemed prepared to say his bit. 'Bibi, we are all aware of what exactly had transpired then. All I can say is, we are truly ashamed of that act.' She bowed before walking towards the waiting vehicle.

Days flew by and soon it was time for her departure. But the old lady was not prepared for her return journey yet. On the last day of her stay at Muzaffarabad, she walked with her sons to the grave of her husband. She sat down beside it and began praying. Her sons sat opposite her and watched her with deep admiration. For a long time, she stayed almost motionless. Only her lips moved. Her children waited and waited. Finally, an hour later, she finished her prayer and gently rested her head on the grave. The brothers too began to stand up but midway realized that their mother's body had become motionless. It didn't take much time for them to realize that she was gone.

Bibi Amrit Kaur was cremated as per Hindu customs and then her ashes were placed in a grave next to her husband's. She wanted it to be her final resting place. Her gravestone was carved with the following words: 'Here lies the mother who was separated from her children by politics. Love and prayer brought them together. May her soul rest in peace.'

One by one, the entire village came to pay obeisance. As the sun began to set, an old man walked in. He was ordinarily dressed and with great effort managed to stand straight near the grave. From his bag, he pulled out an old black burqa and placed it at the grave. With folded hands, he said, 'I was the guard when you arrived at the police chowki and left this burqa outside the door. Please pardon me for my unpardonable act, Bibi.'

It felt as if life had come full circle.

Epilogue

A month later, Mushtaq David, the minister of minority affairs, was arrested for fraudulently sending Pakistanis to Italy. He arranged bail but was soon diagnosed with cancer. Despite the best treatment, he died a painful death in 2010, leaving behind all the ill-gotten wealth he had amassed.

Acknowledgements

I would like to thank the following people:

My parents, for their blessings.

Mr Ajay G. Piramal, for being a solid pillar all through.

My family, for being a great support.

Vaishali Mathur, Saloni Mital, Devangana Dash and Udyotna Kumar of Penguin Random House India, for their support.

Rashmi Bhatnagar, for her inputs.